The Boo
Strong A
Echoe
Examination Room.

Zach couldn't move. He couldn't breathe. He met Mallory's gaze, and they exchanged a long, intimate look. Her eyes were suspiciously bright, and he knew she was close to tears. He felt a fierce protective urge swell in his chest. He had to take care of her and the baby. He *had* to. When he finally found his voice again, it was thick with emotion.

"Is the heartbeat supposed to be that fast?" he asked the doctor.

"Oh, yes. Your baby is perfectly normal," the doctor replied.

Zach exchanged a brief glance with Mallory that dared her to say that it wasn't his baby. She didn't say anything. She couldn't have spoken if her life depended on it. She was listening to the thrilling sound of her baby's heartbeat.

And she had shared it with Zach.

Dear Reader,

Spring is in the air—and all thoughts turn toward love. With six provocative romances from Silhouette Desire, you too can enjoy a season of new beginnings...and happy endings!

Our March MAN OF THE MONTH is Lass Small's *The Best Husband in Texas*. This sexy rancher is determined to win over the beautiful widow he's loved for years! Next, Joan Elliott Pickart returns with a wonderful love story—*Just My Joe*. Watch sparks fly between handsome, wealthy Joe Dillon and the woman he loves.

Don't miss Beverly Barton's new miniseries, 3 BABIES FOR 3 BROTHERS, which begins with *His Secret Child*. The town golden boy is reunited with a former flame—and their child. Popular Anne Marie Winston offers the third title in her BUTLER COUNTY BRIDES series, as a sexy heroine forms a partnership with her lost love in *The Bride Means Business*. Then an expectant mom matches wits with a brooding rancher in Carol Grace's *Expecting*.... And Virginia Dove debuts explosively with *The Bridal Promise,* when star-crossed lovers marry for convenience.

This spring, please write and tell us why you read Silhouette Desire books. As part of our 20th anniversary celebration in the year 2000, we'd like to publish some of this fan mail in the books—so drop us a line, tell us how long you've been reading Desire books and what you love about the series. And enjoy our March titles!

Regards,

Joan Marlow Golan
Senior Editor, Silhouette Desire

Please address questions and book requests to:
Silhouette Reader Service
U.S.: 3010 Walden Ave., P.O. Box 1325, Buffalo, NY 14269
Canadian: P.O. Box 609, Fort Erie, Ont. L2A 5X3

EXPECTING...
CAROL GRACE

SILHOUETTE *Desire*®
Published by Silhouette Books
America's Publisher of Contemporary Romance

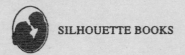

SILHOUETTE BOOKS

ISBN 0-373-76205-4

EXPECTING...

Printed in U.S.A.

CAROL GRACE

has always been interested in travel and living abroad. She spent her junior year in college in France and toured the world working on the hospital ship *Hope*. She and her husband spent the first year and a half of their marriage in Iran, where they both taught English. Then, with their toddler daughter, they lived in Algeria for two years.

Carol says that writing is another way of making her life exciting. Her office is her mountaintop home, which overlooks the Pacific Ocean and which she shares with her inventor husband, their daughter and their son.

One

Mallory pressed the throttle all the way to the floor and willed her small, overloaded car to climb up into the San Rafael Mountains above the university town of San Luis Obispo. Her tires shook and the engine knocked, but that was nothing like the way her hands shook and her knees knocked together. Just a small attack of nerves, she told herself. Understandable, considering this past week she'd quit her teaching job, given up her apartment, packed her meager belongings into her car and was on her way to start a new life. A new life. Oh, Lord, was she ready for this?

She forced herself to look at the scenery, to observe the cattle grazing peacefully beneath majestic oak and stately sycamore trees that dotted the hills on either side. As she passed the sign for the Santa Ynez Valley Ranch she was hit with another panic attack. If the road hadn't been so narrow she might have turned back. Instead she pointed her car toward the imposing California ranch house with the tile roof and the massive overhanging eaves. At the end of the tree-lined entrance, she took a deep breath and got out of her car.

Before she could force herself to walk to the front door and lift the brass knocker, a white-faced calf came charging around the side of the house with a man on horseback in hot pursuit.

"Hey you, get out of the way," he shouted.

Mallory froze with fear. He told her to get out of the way. She told herself to get out of the way. But her body didn't get the message. She stood there, rooted to the spot, her arms out in front of her as if she could stop the runaway calf. She couldn't. She frightened him though. Almost as badly as he frightened her. The animal took one look at her and bolted off in another direction. Reining up, the man glared down at her.

"I thought I told you to get out of the way. You're lucky you weren't run over."

Mallory shaded her eyes, looked up into a sun-bronzed, granite-hard face with flashing blue eyes, and shrugged helplessly. "I'm sorry, but..."

"You're sorry? You would have been even sorrier if a one-hundred-fifty-pound calf had plowed into you. Sorry and unconscious, to boot." He looked over his shoulder and shook his head. "She's gone. Just like the other ones. Do you know how many of these mavericks I've lost in one morning?"

"I have no idea," she said. "I know absolutely nothing about cows. I'm just a...I mean I'm here to—"

"I know why you're here," he said, dismounting and removing his hat. "I just didn't expect you so soon. The hell with the cattle. This is more important. Come on in," he said turning on his heel and walking toward the massive oak front door.

Mallory blinked. So he knew who she was. Then they were even, because she knew who he was too. Everybody knew who Zachary Calhoun was, the biggest cattle rancher in the county, maybe the whole state. Famous for being almost as tough and successful a businessman as his uncle who'd left him the ranch.

It was cool inside the classic Western house, thanks to the thick adobe walls covered with native American weavings. Huge brown leather chairs flanked a massive stone fireplace, the kind you see in ski lodges. Mallory could imagine curling up in one of those chairs with a good book. Or a good man. Which brought her to the reason she was there. It was time to forget the furnishings and ask—

"Now," he said, waving her to a straight-backed chair next to an end table while he leaned against the wall and observed her with his penetrating blue eyes. "We don't have much time, but I need to get a little more information about you."

She bit her lip. She'd heard he was brutally frank. That he didn't mince words. "I'm not sure...I don't know what you already know," she stammered. Not everything. Please don't let him know everything. Not yet. Not today.

"I know you've had some experience. You've done it before, but on a smaller scale."

"That's not true," she said hotly, getting to her feet. "I've never...this is the first time I've ever—"

He raised his hands to stop her from continuing. "Never mind. At this point it doesn't matter. I'm desperate. You're hired."

"What? Wait a minute. This is a mistake. I'm not here about a job. I'm here to see your foreman, Joe Carter. He and I...we're..."

He gave her a cynical smile laced with pity and cut her off. "Sorry, lady, you're a day late. The son-of-a-gun left yesterday. Ran off with the best housekeeper I've ever had, that's why..."

Mallory stared at him. He was still talking, at least his mouth was still moving, but the words were a jumble of sounds. "No notice...irresponsible...unexpected," she heard him say. The blood drained from her head, and the room spun around, as the herbal tea she'd swallowed for breakfast came up and threatened to choke her. Her legs refused to support her any longer, her knees buckled, and the varnished wide-planked floor rose to meet her with a resounding thud. And everything went black.

Zach moved fast, but not fast enough to catch her before she fell. Instead he had to scrape her up off the floor, sweep her into his arms and lay her out on the cool leather couch. He clamped his lips together to keep from blurting out a string of expletives and sat next to her, vigorously rubbing her wrists.

"Wake up," he ordered. "Come on, sweetheart, tell me you're okay. Say you've been sent by the agency to take Diane's place."

Her face was cold and still as a statue. A lump was forming on her head. Cattle he could handle. Sick, well, nervous, skittish, he knew what to do with them. They rarely fainted. And never cried. Women on the other hand were a mystery to him. He'd had little experience dealing with them. His mother had left him to be raised by his uncle. His wife had lasted about six months before she took off. Since then he'd avoided getting involved with the fairer sex.

But his woman problems weren't over yet. Yesterday his superefficient housekeeper ran off with his foreman, and today a strange woman passed out in his living room.

One minute she was standing there, glowing with apparent good health, her long smooth legs in khaki shorts and her white camp shirt buttoned snugly over lush full breasts. If he hadn't noticed these details then, he couldn't have missed them in his brief walk to the couch with her body pressed intimately against his, causing an unmistakable re-action on his part. Now she was out cold. Legs and all. And his body was still throbbing. That was the price of being celibate too long. Damn, damn, damn.

Just when he was about to hire her. Hell, he would have hired Lizzie Borden the ax murderess at this point, he was so desperate. Alarmed at her lack of response, he bent over and put his ear against her left breast to listen to her heart.

What if she never came to? If she went into a coma here on his couch? Thank God her heart was still beating. Just a little too fast. But then so was his. Too fast for comfort. He was about to raise his head from where it was pillowed on her breast, he really was, but before he did she sat up abruptly, as if she'd had electric shock treatment. He got to his feet. Calmly. Deliberately.

"What *were* you doing?" she asked, her eyes wide and alarmed.

He looked down at her with a frown creasing his fore-head. "Checking to see if you were still alive," he said brusquely. "You may not remember but you passed out on my floor here. I was concerned about you. Afraid I might have to call an ambulance. Thought you might have some problem..."

"I have a problem all right," she said, her shoulders suddenly sagging under the weight of some invisible bur-den. "Did you really say Joe had gone somewhere with someone?"

"You got it. He's gone somewhere with someone who was my housekeeper. Who kept order around this place in a hundred different ways. Calmly, efficiently. Did you or did you not come here today to take Diane's place?"

"I didn't. I came to meet Joe. I've got everything I own in my car out there. I thought..."

"Yes?" he said impatiently, noting the color had come back to tinge the woman's cheeks with scarlet. "Spit it out."

"I...I don't know where to start," she said, moving to the edge of the couch and swinging those long lovely legs to the floor.

"Okay," he said crossing his arms over his chest. "I'll start it for you. You were involved with Joe. Stop me if I have it wrong, but I'd say you met him in town, at the Old Town Tavern, listening to one of the R&B bands that rolls through. And he swept you off your feet."

The look on her face told him he'd got it exactly right. It didn't surprise him. What surprised him was that she'd gotten all the way up here. Joe's usual MO was to have a hot and heavy affair with some babe he met in town then break it off just as fast as he'd started it. "Always leave them wanting more," he'd once told Zach with a wicked gleam in his eye one early morning when he'd run into him on his way back to his cabin.

Zach had to hand it to the guy, he never missed a day's work. No matter what he'd been doing the night before. So what happened here? What made Joe take off with Diane, seemingly a sane, sensible, incredibly efficient woman of ordinary looks, leaving this extremely attractive woman high and dry on his couch?

Zach studied the woman before him before continuing. "He told you he loved you. He told you you were beautiful, special... What else?" he prompted.

"He told me he was going to marry me," Mallory said softly. The look on Zachary Calhoun's rugged face told her he thought she was a fool. Not just a fool, a naïve fool. He had no idea just how naïve. And how clueless she was about men. No idea how many years she'd spent with her nose in a book, in classrooms and in libraries. Pursuing knowledge while other girls pursued boys.

He had no idea that a good-looking cowboy with a few sweet words could sweep her off her feet in one night. Make love to her and make her believe he'd marry her. Or maybe he did know. There was something all-seeing in those shrewd blue eyes of Zach's. Something that made her tear her gaze away before he saw the insecurities locked deep inside her.

She couldn't let anyone see the fear that she'd never be desired, never be sought after or fought over the way her sister, Mimi, was. Flirtatious Mimi, the pretty one, who had boys fighting over her from day one and who was now happily married to Mallory's one and only boyfriend. Once he'd seen Mimi that was it, he was gone. It was a long time ago, but still the memory lingered, the old feelings…

Zach stared at her with disbelief. This woman was even more gullible than he thought. He figured she could be as young as twenty with that innocent, classic face and deepset brown eyes, but with those bones she'd look just as pure and pretty at forty. Not that he was looking at her bones. It was the subtle curves he couldn't take his eyes off.

"Well, don't take it personally," he said making an unaccustomed effort to be kind. "If it's any consolation, the guy isn't the marrying type."

Mallory looked at him, her eyes suddenly glazed with unshed tears. His words hadn't helped. She was not consoled.

"You're young. You'll find somebody else," he said heartily. Why on earth would he care if she got married or not? He didn't know her. She would leave in a few minutes and he'd never see her again. Still, he had this irrational urge to try to make her feel better. It must have been those eyes, those sad, dark eyes that threatened to spill over.

"I'm not young," she said. "I'm twenty-eight." She squared her shoulders and blinked back her tears. "I can't believe he didn't even... Maybe he left a note for me."

"Maybe he did," Zach said, tearing his eyes from her soft brown gaze, ignoring the plaintive note in her voice. Anyone dumb enough to fall for Joe didn't deserve pity. They needed professional help. He glanced out the window to see if any of his stray heifers had shown up. No. Today just wasn't his day. It wasn't as disastrous as yesterday; today it was just plain terrible.

"Don't get your hopes up," he said. "But if you feel like it, you could walk down to his place and have a look around."

She stood up quickly, then rocked back on her heels.

He grabbed her by the elbow, forcibly steadying her with his hand. "I'll walk with you," he said. "All I need is for you to get lost between here and there, to pass out again and not be found for days, which would cause me even more headaches than I have already." He was sick of Joe's profligate ways, sick of dealing with an ineffective employment agency, of losing employees and replacing them with others.

"I'm sorry," she said trying to pull her arm free from his grasp, but he was not about to let her go. He was afraid she'd faint again. She was, too. Though she'd never fainted before in her life, lately she was doing all kinds of things she'd never done before. Drinking too much. Flirting with a stranger, the first randy cowboy to cross her path. Then going to bed with him. And next quitting her job, making wedding plans and changing her life. It all started on her birthday when her colleagues at the university had taken her out to the tavern to celebrate. That's when she'd met Joe. It was a brief fling. Her first. And her last.

"Not as sorry as I am," he muttered as they walked down the path together. When they reached the cabin, Zach threw the door open and held it while she looked around.

"Nice place," he commented. "No wonder everyone on the ranch is bugging me about it. Before the sheets are cold they all want to move in. Diane had some system for deciding who had first claim, but I'll be damned if I know what it was."

Mallory wasn't listening to him. She wandered from the small cozy living room with a potbellied woodstove and a braid rug to the kitchen with rustic tiles and a view of the surrounding hills. Then to the wood-paneled bedroom with a king-size bed, the striped sheets left in a tangle. This was the cabin she'd been going to live in. The bed she'd been going to sleep in. With him. Her face flamed. From shame. From humiliation. Before she left the room she took a deep breath and held her head high. She would not let that man with the all-knowing look in his cool blue eyes and the foul temper see her weak side again. Or try to make her feel better with empty words and clichés.

When she returned to the living room he was holding a white envelope in his hand. "You were right," he admitted. "He left you a note. That is, if you're Mallory Phillips."

She snatched it out of his hand and read it standing up. Joe said he was sorry, but marriage, even to someone as wonderful as her, was not in the cards for him now or ever. He wished her good luck in her career. Her heart plummeted. He was talking about the career she'd just put on hold to join him here, to marry him and have a—

"Good news? Bad news?" Zach asked with a curious look in his eyes.

She stared at the letter for a long moment, while the tears welled up and threatened to spill down her cheeks. She would not cry in front of Zachary Calhoun. She could feel his eyes on her, watching, waiting, expecting the worst from her. Well this time he wasn't going to get it. When she looked up she'd arranged her mouth into a stiff smile and held her tears firmly in check.

"Neither," she said briskly, tucking the letter in her breast pocket. "Just an explanation." She brushed past him on her way out the door, aware of his rock-hard chest muscles, of his washboard-flat stomach and the earthy scent of leather and tobacco.

Her hands trembled. Heat shimmied up her spine. It had nothing to do with Zach and his blatant masculinity. It had everything to do with her and her heightened awareness of all things sensual—sights and sounds and tastes and smells and feelings, too. Like the way his head had felt pressed against her breast. Hormones, that's all it was. Hormonal overload.

Out in the sunshine she took a deep breath. "I'm fine now," she assured him when he joined her. "I won't trouble you anymore." She turned and started up the path.

He grabbed her by the shoulders and turned her around to face him. "Where are you going?" he asked.

"Home," she said, forgetting she had no home to go to.

"Where's that? I thought you had everything you own in your car."

She sighed. "I do."

"Ever been a housekeeper?"

"No."

"Ever wanted to be?"

"Absolutely not."

"What are you?"

"I'm an astronomer."

He dropped his hands from her shoulders. He raised his eyebrows, radiating skepticism from every pore. Either he didn't believe her or she'd surprised him. She guessed he was a man who wasn't that easily surprised. But she'd done it. That gave her some satisfaction on a day that hadn't offered much else.

"You think you know a lot about women, don't you?" she asked.

He shook his head. His eyes shuttered. "I don't know anything about them." Then abruptly he changed the subject. "Were you going to watch the stars from up here?" he asked.

"The nebulae. That's my field. I thought it would be a good place with the altitude, and no ambient light or pollutants in the air to interfere." She glanced with longing at the green hills that undulated to the horizon and drew in a breath of pure, clean air.

"What do you think now?" he asked, absently chewing on a piece of grass.

"It would have been a good place," she admitted.

"Got your own telescope?"

"A hundred-pound reflector telescope. With a tripod. It's small but has good light-gathering power for its size."

"Then stay here. Be my housekeeper during the day and watch your damned nebulae at night. Which is what you should have been doing instead of fooling around with my foreman."

Her face flamed. The man just didn't know when to quit. "I wouldn't be your housekeeper if you paid me."

"But I will pay you. More than you make as an astronomer. Enough to buy yourself a really big telescope."

She felt herself waver. Picturing a new telescope, one that could peer all the way to intergalactic nebulae. How hard could it be to keep somebody's house anyway? "What does it entail?" she asked. "Making beds, cooking meals?"

He shook his head. "This is a big ranch. We have a cook, and we have maids. That cabin you saw was one of many. The housekeeper knows who lives where, which ones need repairs, she orders supplies, does the household budget, and God knows what else. I'm gone a fair amount so I need someone to keep everything in order inside the house. That's what Diane did. She was remarkable."

He knew she was vacillating. He pressed on. "No physical work, all administrative. If you can keep track of a few million stars, you can handle a few dozen employees, their housing, their meals, the main house, some entertaining and a thousand acres of ranchland, can't you?"

"A thousand?"

"Forget the thousand acres. Forget the ranchland. The foreman handles that. Or at least my new one will. I'll have someone unload your car. Your suite is in the main house."

Mallory could have said no then. She could have gone to her car and instead of unloading it she could have driven back to town. And then what? She'd declined to teach summer session, preferring to do research. Hoping to publish her results and get her appointment changed from assistant professor to associate. She'd given up her apartment. Didn't have much money. And then there was the real reason she'd come up here. The reason she'd decided to get married. The one she hadn't mentioned and wouldn't, not until she had to.

By mid-afternoon she'd stashed all her gear in a suite that was larger than her whole apartment in town. Her clothes were divided between a pine chest and a spacious walk-in closet, her computer and her boxes of journals on the oak desk. Her telescope and tripod stood in the corner of the sitting room formerly occupied by Diane, her predecessor. She'd met Juana, a maid, George, a handyman and Tex the cook, in his restaurant-size kitchen.

"You like barbecued beef?" Tex had asked giving his spicy sauce a stir.

"Love it," she'd told him, as her stomach churned. She used to love it, but recently the only thing she could get down was saltine crackers.

"Miss Diane said my sauce was the best she'd ever eaten. You a friend of hers?"

"No, no, I didn't know her."

"Fine woman. Hard worker. Can't believe she'd run off like that. Shocked us all. Now Joe, nothin' he could do would shock us."

Mallory gulped. She wondered when the talk would die down, if ever. Would she always be only a poor replacement for Diane? Always? There was no always. Not for her. She'd be lucky if she lasted the summer, considering the personality of her boss. A summer should give her time to figure out what to do next. Depending on what shape her research was in, and of course what shape she was in. In the mean time she had Diane's job while Diane had *her* man.

"Dinner's at seven," Tex said. "Hope you're not on a diet like Diane was."

So Diane was fat. Or was she thin? Whatever she was, she had something Joe wanted and Mallory didn't. Strange how fast she had accepted the fact. Much faster than she'd accepted her sister's taking her boyfriend away. As if she'd had a choice either time. Funny how the shock was wearing off already. And how fast Joe's classic cowboy face was fading from her memory.

She had not seen any more of her boss, not since he'd told her what the obscenely large salary was, shaken her hand and pointed to a large, richly appointed room he called "the office" in one wing of the sprawling house.

"That's where we meet every morning. In the meantime..."

Just as she was about to tell him she couldn't do anything in the meantime except collapse and that she was having second thoughts about being anybody's housekeeper and especially his, someone yelled to him from outside the house that the vet had arrived, and he disappeared. She staggered to her room and lay on the bed, wondering how she'd ever sleep a wink in the same bed as the woman who'd taken Joe away from her and spoiled her plans.

Yet she did sleep, until dinner. Another weird thing, along with her heightened sensory awareness was her need for an afternoon nap. Of course, staying up late tracking the cosmos could do that to a person. But it never had done that to her before. She felt better after she'd had a shower and changed into khaki pants and a soft cotton shirt.

The pungent smell of Tex's barbecue wafted through the covered walkway that led to the large, cheerful dining room. When she opened the door, the dozen or more people at the table stopped talking. Heads swerved in her direction. A hush fell over the room. Everyone was staring at her, everyone but her boss. He was busy piling potato salad on his plate. He already knew what she looked like, both conscious and unconscious.

A tall, tanned older man with a sweeping mustache

stood and doffed his hat. "I know you must be, but you *can't* be our new housekeeper."

"Why can't I be?" she asked, sitting in the only vacant chair, next to the dashing older man.

"Much too young and much too pretty. Thought you'd learned your lesson, Zach."

Zach looked up briefly, just long enough to meet her gaze. If she expected warmth and support, she didn't get it. There was only a brief flicker of recognition, as if he'd almost forgotten he'd even hired her.

"This *is* our new housekeeper," he said briskly. "Mallory, meet the staff." He proceeded to go around the table, introducing his vet, his mechanic, the buyer, his business manager and so forth until the names and faces all blurred together. Except for Perry, the man who thought she was too young and pretty to be a housekeeper.

"Tell me," Perry said slanting his head in her direction. "What's a nice girl like you doing on a ranch like this?"

"Just what Mr. Calhoun said," she replied, taking a small piece of barbecued brisket from a platter served by a young woman in blue jeans and a braid over one shoulder. "I'm the new housekeeper." Maybe if she said it often enough she'd start to believe it. *I'm* the new housekeeper, I'm the new *housekeeper*, I *am* the new—

"And what do you think of *Mr.* Calhoun?" Perry asked over the din of renewed conversation and the clatter of silverware.

"He's…very decisive," she said with a brief glance toward the end of the table. "Seems to know what he wants."

"That he does," Perry agreed, shaking hot pepper onto his baked potato. "But what he wants is not always what he needs."

"I see," she said. But she didn't see at all. Anyone as

rich and successful as Zach Calhoun could surely get anything he wanted or needed. Case in point. He needed a
housekeeper, so he'd gotten her, using his forceful personality and an outlandish salary. If it hadn't been her, it
would have been the next hapless female who'd happened
to pull up in his driveway for whatever reason. To marry
his foreman or deliver a truckload of gravel. It didn't seem
to matter. He was just looking for a warm body.

"I guess you heard what happened to your predecessor?" he asked.

"Do you mean..."

"I mean she ran off with our foreman, and no one even
knew they were involved. Talk about the odd couple. It's
the biggest scandal to happen around here in a long time.
No one understands why they left, why they had to run
off. Why didn't she just move in with him and stay here
and keep her job?"

"I don't know," Mallory said. But she did know. It was
because Mallory was coming to marry Joe. And he didn't
want to marry her. Not at all. He didn't want to marry her
so much that he took the housekeeper and left a good
steady job just to avoid her. And that hurt.

"They'll never find anyone like Zach to work for," he
observed, filling her water glass for her. "He's tough but
he's fair. By the way," he said bending his head so close
his mustache tickled her ear. "Has anyone been given
Joe's cabin, do you know? Maybe you could put me on
top of the list. Perry's the name. *Perry.*"

"I'll remember," she said, leaning forward to avoid his
hand on the back of her chair. Was it the housekeeper's
job to assign housing? To fend off lecherous old wranglers?

"You're not worried about filling Diane's rather large
shoes, are you?"

Large shoes. Was that just a saying or did Diane really have big feet? "Well, yes," she said, "now that you mention it, I am worried. I hear she was quite good at...what she did."

"Good? She was the best. You had much experience?"

She took a sip from her water glass. "Yes and no," she hedged.

He smiled as if he saw right through her. As if he knew she'd been hired off the street, or off the floor as it were.

"Yes, our boss appears to have everything," Perry said, returning to the subject he'd begun. "And he does. Except in his personal life. I'm talking about a wife and a family, of course. You married?"

"No." She glanced at the man at the end of the table. Up to now she'd avoided looking at him. Afraid of what? That he might have the power to see into her soul? Find out her secret? The man who oozed wealth and self-confidence was at that moment glaring at her. Even down the length of the table she could feel his disapproval. Of what? What had she done but nibble on some barbecued beef and listen to Perry gossip?

The conversation at Zach's end of the table revolved around topics like shorthorns and Brahmans. So even at dinner he was all business. But he was all macho man, too. In control of his house, his land and his personnel. Except for one renegade ex-foreman and one ex-housekeeper. Was that the reason for the frown on his face? Or was it directed at her personally?

"Does he have a wife and family?" she asked.

"No," Perry said, stuffing a large piece of beef into his mouth. "That's my point. What good is all this land and money if you've got no one to share it with?"

Leaving Perry's question hanging in the air, she stared at Zach, wondering if he felt the same way. If he did, there must be a ton of women who would jump at the chance to share this beautiful place. If they could ignore his acerbic personality, his male chauvinist ideas and his domineering manner.

Mrs. Calhoun would have her meals cooked for her, her bed made and acres of wildflowers and stables of horses to call her own. Or half her own. If he could talk an astronomer into being a housekeeper in one half hour, he could certainly talk any other woman into being his wife. If he wanted one. She wondered if he wanted children. She never had. Not until now.

At that precise moment he looked up and caught her staring at him. Their glances met and held for a long minute while the conversation dimmed in the background and the faces around the table faded. She tried to break the contact but she couldn't. His intense gaze held her captive over bowls of creamed corn and platters of tomatoes. She'd already consented to be his housekeeper. What more did he want with her? Her stomach knotted with nerves and apprehension. She shredded her napkin in her lap without realizing it.

Just as she thought she might have to make an abrupt departure from the table to escape his brilliant blue gaze, his interest in her faded as the maid brought in coffee and plates of freshly baked spice cookies and someone asked Zach if he'd ever found his missing calves.

Before she'd left the dining room, two more people asked if they could have Joe's cabin. She said she'd see. She'd say anything to get out of there and away from the aura of the presence at the end of the table. But just as she was the last to arrive in the dining room, she was the last to leave. Or next to last. Zach was still at the table, making notes on a paper napkin. Without realizing she was doing it, she held her breath and tiptoed past him.

His arm snaked out and grabbed her hand. "Not so fast."

"What, what is it?" she gasped.

"Sit down."

She sat.

"I want to talk to you."

"Go ahead." Her heart was pounding. Not from fear. From apprehension. Anxiety. Misgivings.

He pressed her hands between his rough callused palms. "Your hands are like ice."

"Cold hands, warm heart," she said lightly.

"That's right. I remember," he said deliberately, letting his heated gaze follow the curve of her breasts and linger there. Her face flamed. She tugged at her hands. He held on.

"Just a warning. Stay away from Perry. He's a lech. Unless you want to end up like your predecessor."

"I don't intend to run away with one of your staff," she said coolly. Little did he know she was not the type to inspire such passion in anyone. The brief affair with Joe was her one-and-only fling. His interest in her had so surprised and flattered her she'd lost her normal good sense. Of course she could blame the three beers or the music or the fact that it was the night of her twenty-eighth birthday and she was still a virgin. A reluctant virgin. There was all that. And there was more. The need to prove she could attract a man like Joe.

"That's reassuring. Who do you intend to run away with?"

"No one. By the way," she said, looking down at his broad, work-hardened hands that still clasped her pale slender fingers. "Am I on duty twenty-four hours a day?"

"Of course not. I wouldn't dream of interfering with your stargazing."

"They're not stars, they're nebulae. Clouds made of gas and smoke and…"

"Whatever."

She pushed her chair out from the table. Enough of this patronizing boor.

With a loud scraping sound he pulled the chair with her in it back to the table and said, "I'm not through with you yet."

Two

He poured her a cup of coffee from the urn on the table, leaned back in his chair and observed her through narrowed eyes.

She shook her head and set the cup aside.

"How are you going to stay awake for the Milky Way if you don't get some caffeine in your system?" he asked.

"I'm not staying awake for the Milky Way. The Milky Way is a galaxy, made up of stars, of which we are all a part, the nebulae, however—"

"Are clouds made of gas and smoke."

"And dust. Very good," she said with grudging admiration.

"I took notes. Thought there might be a quiz," he said. "Here's an idea. Instead of studying those nebulae of yours, why don't you find a new comet and name it after yourself? Mallory Phillips. It has a nice ring to it."

∴"I'll think about it," she said. The way he rolled her name around on his tongue made a shiver go up her spine.

"Tea?" he asked.

She capitulated. "All right." If she wasn't going to get away from him anytime soon she might as well have a cup of tea.

∴She thought he'd have someone bring it. Instead he went to the kitchen himself and came back five minutes later with a cup of fragrant, passion peach.

She eyed him over her steaming cup. "Don't you have...things to do?"

"I have to talk to you. About avoiding the men here."

"I don't see how I can do that and still do my job," she said. "What is my job, by the way? I know, housekeeper. But what does that mean, actually, besides supervising? Supervising who, what, how? How am I supposed to supervise people who know more than I do? Maybe this isn't such a good idea."

"You're just nervous," he said. "It's a great idea."

He *would* say that since it was his idea.

"Not just supervising...coordinating," he corrected.

"All right, coordinating. What do I coordinate?"

"Everything. Everybody. You'll learn on the job. You'll ask people who've been here awhile. You'll find Diane's household records. Learn where she ordered supplies and groceries and how she assigned housing and who does what around here. Not all at once. As you go along. The important thing is that you not..."

"I know. Run away with your foreman. Don't worry, it's not likely to happen again. Not to me, anyway. I've never been... As you said, I'm a day late."

Zach rubbed his hand over his forehead. "You're not the only one. Day two and the agency still can't find anybody for me to even interview. How do they expect me to run a thousand-acre ranch without a foreman?'' he asked.

"Isn't two days a little short notice?'' she asked. "If you're so impatient why don't you just wait for the next man to pull up to your house and hire him?''

"Like I did you? I'll remind you that I thought they'd sent you. And you did nothing to convince me otherwise.''

"I fainted,'' she said taking a sip of the soothing, hot beverage. "That should have tipped you off.''

"Good point. Housekeepers don't faint. At least Diane never did.''

"Diane this and Diane that. I'm not Diane. I'm not even a housekeeper.''

"You are now,'' he said flatly. "It can't be that hard. But a foreman is another matter. I want someone who's had experience running a large ranch. They're out there, I know they are. I just can't seem to get my hands on one. I don't expect to get someone like Joe. Whatever his character flaws, he was damned good at what he did.''

Mallory thought of the night she'd met him. His handsome face, his smooth talk, his expertise on the tiny dance floor, plying her with drinks, seducing her with words as well as action in that small hotel room across the road from the bar. Yes, he was damned good at what he did. And she was an admirer, and a willing participant. She couldn't blame Joe. She'd gone willingly, like a moth to the flame.

"What's the matter?'' Zach said, studying her flushed face.

She picked up her cup and took a large gulp of tea. "Nothing.''

"Were you in love with him?''

"No, of course not.''

"Then why were you going to marry him?''

"You wouldn't understand,'' she said.

"Try me."

She brushed her hand across her cheek. "I don't know. I mean...maybe I was in love. I know, people don't usually get married unless...unless they have a good reason. But what is love, anyway? What does it feel like?" She wished she *had* been in love. She wished that had been the reason for those wedding plans. And love would have excused her behavior in that hotel room. She really did want to know about love. Just because Zach wasn't married didn't mean he didn't have the answer. Anyone who looked as worldly-wise as he did and was as rich and good-looking as he was had probably been in love dozens of times.

"Damned if I know," he said, rocking his chair back against the wall and folding his arms behind his head. "You're asking the wrong person. I don't think you've answered *my* question yet. If you didn't know if you were in love, why did you want to get married?"

She set her cup down with a thud. "That's none of your business." She'd had all the questions she could handle for one day. If she could summon the energy to walk out, she would. But right now she was drained.

Zach sat at the table, crumpling the napkin with the formula for feed he'd scribbled on it. He looked at her cup and noted the imprint of her lips on the rim. If she wasn't sitting there staring off into space he would have picked it up and held it to his mouth. To taste passion peach blended with her own elusive scent.

He still didn't get it. Why in the hell would she want to marry a promiscuous stud like Joe if she didn't love him? Then suddenly he did get it. Because he was a stud, of course. Even Diane couldn't resist him. So why should a beautiful woman like Mallory?

Tex came in and set a fresh pot of coffee in front of them.

"More tea, Ms. Mallory?" he asked.

She shook her head. She looked like she wanted to leave but was too tired to move. To break the silence Zach turned to Tex. "You've been married, Tex, you know anything about love?" Zach asked.

Tex wiped his hands on his apron. "I know this much. It makes the world go round."

"Thanks," Zach said drily.

"What're you asking me for? You been married yourself, boss."

"That was a long time ago."

"Once you've been in love, you never forget how it was," Tex said.

"Then I couldn't have been in love, because I *have* forgotten," Zach said, drumming his knuckles on the table. "All I remember is the shock when she told me she was leaving."

Mallory looked up and met his gaze. There was sympathy in her dark eyes. And he knew he'd said too much. He didn't want sympathy from anybody, especially from a woman he didn't even know.

"Well," he said, "it's been a long day. You're probably tired." If she didn't take the hint that it was time for her to leave, he'd be surprised.

But she didn't, and he *was* surprised to hear her say to Tex, "I think I will have another cup of tea."

The cook smiled and took her cup to refill it.

"How long have you had the ranch?" Mallory asked.

He paused. He didn't really want to talk about himself. But he could hardly ignore a direct question, either. "My uncle died seven or eight years ago. But I've lived here since I can remember. I was about ten when my mother dumped me here and took off.''

"Dumped you?'' she asked.

"Call it what you want. I don't blame her for taking off. As a single mother she was at the end of her rope. It hurt at the time, but leaving me here with my uncle was the best thing she could have done. For her and for me. I know everybody doesn't feel this way, or they wouldn't keep quitting, but I love this place. Better than anything.''

"Better than anybody?'' she asked.

"Yeah, why? There's nothing wrong with that. The only thing that's wrong is that I can't run it alone. I depend on others. I need good help. Yesterday I lost two of the best.''

"Today you replaced one of 'em,'' Tex said from the doorway, nodding at Mallory. How long had he been standing there? Not that it mattered, he knew more about Zach than anybody.

"Did I do the right thing?'' Zach asked with a wry glance at Mallory.

"She looks good to me,'' the cook said.

"She looks tired to me,'' Zach said, noting her drooping eyelids.

"You're right,'' Mallory said with a yawn. "She's going to bed. Good night.'' She rose from the table, leaving her tea untouched, and walked out the dining room door.

"Pretty little thing,'' Tex noted, crossing his arms across his ample waist.

Little? He hadn't picked her up off the floor and carried her across the room. "Doesn't have any experience,'' Zach said, pouring Tex a cup of coffee.

"Then why...''

"I don't know,'' Zach said. But he knew why he'd hired her. It was because he couldn't send her away. Because there was something in those limpid brown eyes that told him she needed help, a place to go. It was the tears that she fought to hold in check that called forth his grudging admiration, and the way she handled the shock of hearing Joe was gone. By fainting, yes. But when she recovered, with fortitude and grim determination. Those things showed her mettle.

"I'm running a business, you know," Zach reminded himself as well as Tex. "Not a home for the lovelorn or an observatory for astronomers."

"Who?" Tex asked, sitting in a chair halfway down the table.

Zach took a swallow of hot coffee. "She's an astronomer," he said.

"She gonna read our horoscope?" Tex asked.

"Afraid not," Zach said, not wanting to go into the difference between astronomy and astrology. "I wasn't going to tell anybody she's not a housekeeper, but you're not just anybody. You've been with me for the last nine years. Making food that keeps a lot of guys around when they might have had reason to leave."

"Thank you, boss," Tex said.

"You're welcome."

"They can look into the future, you know," Tex said.

"Who can?"

"Astrologers. They can tell if money or romance is in your future," Tex said.

"I don't need an astrologer to tell me that romance is not in my future. I tried it once. It didn't work."

"Maybe it's time you tried again," Tex suggested.

Zach did a double take. He looked into the cook's friendly dark eyes. "Me, try again? Have you been into the cooking sherry?" Zach asked. "As if I didn't have enough problems. As if I didn't have goals which don't include anything but raising the best beef cattle in the state. Now you want me to go out looking for romance?''

"Not go out looking. Just, you know, don't fight it."

Zach stared at the man. In all these years he'd never had a personal talk like this with him. Now all of a sudden Tex was talking to him like a Dutch uncle. Though Zach's real uncle had never talked like this, either. He was a cool, tough rancher who hadn't known what to say to the boy he'd raised.

"If she's not a housekeeper, why'd you hire her?" Tex asked.

"I don't know." Zach raked his hand through his hair. "I was desperate. I thought she'd been sent."

"Maybe she was," Tex suggested. "By the angels."

"I meant by the agency." He didn't say that he'd had a strange, irrational urge to protect her. Because when he heard she'd fallen for the likes of Joe, he somehow knew he had to keep her from falling for the next randy cowboy who came along.

"Maybe it was a mistake hiring her," Zach said. "I'm probably gonna have to let her go."

Tex frowned and stood up. "Don't do anything till you read your horoscope tomorrow," he warned. "Or you'll be sorry."

The next morning Mallory stood at the entrance of the walk-in closet and realized she had nothing in her wardrobe that vaguely resembled what a housekeeper would wear. Couldn't the super-wonderful Diane have left behind one housekeeper outfit? One powder-blue polyester shirt and pants would have done it, preferably with an elastic waist. Along with a set of instructions as to how to be a housekeeper. But the closet had been cleaned out. And Mallory's clothes were either trim skirts she'd worn while teaching that didn't seem to fit anymore or warm pants for stargazing. So she dug out a pair of baggy cotton shorts from the bottom of her duffel bag and a T-shirt to wear to the ten o'clock meeting.

Not that it mattered. He wasn't there.

"He's going to town to raise a little hell with the job agency," Mike the mechanic told her. "Feels he's not getting enough attention from them. Said he's not coming back till they find him a foreman. Can't run a ranch without a foreman. Boss's getting impatient. He's got no foreman. So, no meeting today."

"But..." She looked around in desperation. What was she supposed to do? How was she supposed to do it? She thought he'd brief her today.

"Boss said he wants to see you this afternoon."

"This afternoon? I'm not waiting around until afternoon to talk to him. I want to see him now."

Mike pointed out the window where Zach was cleaning the windshield of his racy black sports car. "There he is. Don't blink or you'll miss him."

Mallory dashed past the mechanic and out the front door. Zach was just easing his tall frame into the front seat. "Wait a minute," she yelled. She didn't wait for him to answer, she went back in the house, grabbed her purse and jacket from her room and went back outside.

He turned to look in her direction, his face expressionless, as if he'd never seen her before, never heard her yell at him to wait, and started the motor. She yanked the passenger door open.

"Wait a minute. I was expecting a meeting. I need to talk to you."

"Later," he said brusquely.

"No, now. I'm the housekeeper, right? I'm supposed to housekeep, but I don't know what to do or how to do it."

He exhaled loudly and impatiently. "Don't do anything. Relax. We'll talk about it when I get back."

"I can't relax. I'm a believer in the Puritan work ethic. If I'm working for you I'm going to work. But I can't work if I don't know what to do. I want to talk about it now."

"I'm going to town now."

"Then I'll go with you," she said, climbing into the seat next to him. "I have some shopping to do. We can talk along the way."

He shook his head. She fastened her seat belt with a loud click.

"Okay," he said, racing the motor. "But when we get there, you're on your own. I've got business to attend to."

"I know. At the job agency."

He headed down the driveway without speaking. She looked out the window. She'd said she wanted to talk, but now that she was sitting next to him, the smell of leather upholstery mingling with his citrus aftershave, she couldn't think of anything to say. Her mind was blank. The questions that were burning to be asked were all forgotten.

Her body was buzzing with awareness. Awareness of his oxford cloth shirt with the sleeves rolled up revealing muscular sun-bronzed arms. His strong, capable hands on the steering wheel. This idea of riding into town with him was not a good one. Sitting so close she had goose bumps on her bare arms. She was acting too much on impulse these days, unable to think logically. She had half a mind to tell him to stop and let her out, that she'd walk back.

But he distracted her with a question. "So who's responsible for laying this work ethic on you?"

"My grandparents."

"They lived with you?"

"No, we lived with them. They were wonderful. Hard-working, old-fashioned in some ways, but understanding, too.''

''What about your parents?''

''My father was in the foreign service. Two years here, two years there. At first they sent us back in the summers to Grandma Annie and Grandpa Ted's, my sister and I, but the schools were iffy and Mimi and I were tired of moving all the time, making new friends, changing schools. So finally we came back to live with them year-round in Arizona. Grandpa had a small telescope set up in the backyard. I guess that's where I got the idea I wanted to be an astronomer.''

He nodded.

''But that's not what I wanted to talk about,'' she said. ''It's about the job.''

''Must have taken a lot of hard work and study to get the job, and years of graduate school.''

''That's where the work ethic came in handy,'' she explained. ''But that's not the job I mean.''

''What classes do you teach?''

''Three sections of Astronomy 101 and an advanced seminar. I really like the freshmen best,'' she said, turning to face him, enthusiasm spilling from her voice. ''Taking them out the first night with a map of the sky. We plot the stars and the planets. The best part is to see the students get excited.''

''The way you did when you looked into your grandfather's telescope.''

She studied his profile, the high cheekbones and the broad forehead. She didn't expect someone who'd seemed so self-centered to also be intuitive. ''Yes. How did you know?'' she asked.

He shrugged and asked some more questions, which she answered. But she never got a chance to discuss her duties at all. When they arrived, he pulled into a parking space on the main street.

"Meet you back at the car, in what...two hours?" he suggested.

"Fine," she said.

Zach burst into the placement office on the third floor of the only high-rise in town. The name on the door said "Frank Lovejoy and Associates. Personnel and Consulting. Specializing in Ranch and Country." The receptionist looked up and murmured, "Uh-oh," as he brushed by her on his way to see Frank, the president, founder and CEO.

"Gotta have a foreman, Frank, and I've got to have one today," he said, pounding on the man's desk. A greeting in this case was superfluous.

"What about the housekeeper? I might have a housekeeper for you." Frank ignored Zach's display of temper and shoved a manila folder across his desk.

Zach hesitated. He'd had a restless night. Thinking about her. The way her face paled when he told her Joe had gone. The way her hands felt captured between his. Her face pressed against his chest as he carried her to the couch. The glow in her eyes when she talked about her nebulae. He scoffed at horoscopes, but Tex's warning lingered in his ears. "Don't do anything...or you'll be sorry."

Zach leafed through the folder. The housekeeper was fifty-five years old. Hobbies were knitting and bridge. Came highly recommended. She sounded ideal. He didn't need to read his horoscope to know she was right for the job.

"I'll take her," Zach said. Mallory would understand. She was already having second thoughts. In fact, she was so concerned about the job, she'd ridden into town with him just to talk about it. Of course she'd understand she couldn't do the job.

"Don't you want to interview her?"

"Not necessary," he said shrugging off a twinge of guilt. "Now about a foreman."

"I heard what happened," Frank said, shaking his head.

"Hasn't everyone?" Zach asked, irritably. He was trying to be patient. While the whole town was gossiping about his foreman and his housekeeper, all he could think of was how he was going to tell Mallory she was fired.

You can keep the advance, he'd say. *Keep the first month's salary. But you can't stay. I don't know what I was thinking. You were right. You can't supervise people who know more than you do. Not that you don't know a lot. It's just in the wrong field. If you'd majored in housekeeping instead of astronomy...*

No, that wouldn't do.

It's nothing personal, he'd say. Like hell it wasn't. It was nothing *but* personal. Personal because of the way she appealed to his protective instincts. Instincts he didn't know he had. Instincts he didn't want to have.

"There must be a foreman in there somewhere," Zach said, gesturing toward the file drawer. "Or better yet, out there." He gestured toward the window, toward the hills beyond the town.

"No doubt, but... Hey, I got an idea for you. Only thing is he's in semiretirement. You'll have to talk him into coming back to work."

"How old is he?"

"Ageless."

"Don't tell me it's Slim Perkins."

"It is."

"The guy is almost ninety if he's a day."

"So? You some kind of ageist?"

"No, but this is hard work."

"Give him a try."

Zach exhaled loudly. "Okay. Send him out. Send them both out. As soon as possible."

"Nice doing business with you, Zach. As usual." Frank stood and shook Zach's hand.

"Yeah, right."

Zach felt a profound sense of relief as he walked down the main street in the charming town of San Luis Obispo, past the historic white-walled mission built by the missionary Father Serra in 1772, while the bell from the tourist trolley clanged as it clattered past.

To celebrate he walked into his favorite restaurant to have lunch. The ranch would get along without him for another hour or two, he thought, buying the local newspaper to read while he ate. But he never got a chance to read it. Mallory was seated all by herself in a big booth. If he'd thought fast enough he could have turned around and walked out the minute he saw her dark head bent over the menu. Or pretended not to see her and taken a seat at the counter.

But he didn't. His feet took him to her booth as if he was a robot programmed to go wherever she was.

"Mallory," he said briskly, taking the bench opposite her.

Her eyes widened. "Found your foreman already?" she asked.

"Yes." Now was the time to tell her he'd found a housekeeper also, but he didn't. The waitress came, and he ordered clam chowder. She ordered a tuna melt and iced tea. Then he leaned back against the vinyl seat and studied her, trying to figure out why she looked different. Was it the crisp striped tunic she wore? Or her short hair, feathered around her face? Whatever it was, she looked younger in this hairstyle, and totally defenseless. And totally impossible to fire. Damn, damn, damn.

He frowned. "You look different."

"I had my hair cut and I went shopping," she said. "Do I look more like a housekeeper?"

He shook his head. "Hardly," he said. Her face fell.

He reached across the table, tilted her chin with his thumb so he could look in her eyes. The hurt she tried to hide caused his stomach muscles to tense. "That was a compliment," he said. "Don't worry, okay?"

She nodded, but he hadn't convinced her. He could tell by the way she was studying the wine list upside down. If anyone was worried, it should be him. He'd just hired two housekeepers. Yesterday he had none, today he had two. Maybe that was best. Then if one ran off with the foreman, he'd have a spare. No, that was ridiculous. His fifty-five-year-old housekeeper running off with his octogenarian foreman? Not likely. Considering her background and his age, probably neither did a whole lot of running. He had to fire Mallory.

He told himself she wouldn't mind. That she'd never wanted the job to begin with. And she was worried about what it entailed. She'd probably found out for herself by now that she didn't belong at the ranch—look how fast she wangled a ride back to town today—and she would welcome the chance to get out of it. Where would she go? Back where she came. What would she do? Keep watching those dust clouds. Better than sweeping them out of corners.

"Have a nice morning?" he asked, trying to bring the conversation to a strictly impersonal level.

"Yes. I bought a few things," she said.

"Like your new shirt there." His eyes followed the modest neckline and the buttons that ran down the front.

"Yes." She flushed and she ran her finger around the collar. "I wanted to get something... What do housekeepers wear, anyway? What did Diane wear?"

"I have no idea," he said. She'd worked for him for six years and he couldn't picture anything she wore. At all. Ever.

"Was she pretty?" Mallory asked.

"You got me." He opened a packet of crackers and crumbled them into his soup.

She sipped her iced tea. "You don't have to spare my feelings," she said. "If she was pretty, say so."

"I tell you I didn't notice. What does it matter if she was Miss California? The important thing was that she was good at her job."

"I thought if I looked like a housekeeper, I'd be able to act like one. Then someday I might be as good as Diane."

"I wouldn't worry about that," he said, avoiding her gaze. If ever there was a time to tell her, it was now. *You don't need to look like a housekeeper, because you're not going to be one. You wouldn't have liked the job, anyway. It's a lot of work. The kind of work you're not used to.* But he didn't say that. He didn't have a chance.

"Don't tell me what to worry about," she said under her breath as the waitress refilled her iced tea glass. "You have no idea what I'm really worried about."

"No, I don't," he said, struck by the way her voice shook just slightly. He leaned forward, his soup forgotten. "Do you want to tell me?"

"Zach Calhoun, I thought that was you. Mind if I join you?" Before he could say yes he did mind, a tall woman lavishly decorated in silver and turquoise jewelry squeezed into the booth next to him and looked up expectantly at Mallory. Just when Mallory was going to tell him what was bothering her. He glared at the woman and stifled his irritation.

"How are you, Stella?" he asked. "Do you know Mallory...Mallory..."

"Phillips," Mallory said.

Stella stuck her hand across the table to shake Mallory's. "Nice to meet you." Then she turned to Zach. "I heard about your foreman," she blurted, unable to contain a knowing smile.

Oh, Lord, he should have known. Ranchers who hadn't had much to say to him for years would now take the opportunity to gloat over his misfortune in losing Joe.

"Did you really?" he asked. He wished she wouldn't bring this up in front of Mallory. But how was Stella to know she'd been jilted by Joe?

"The word is he got his girlfriend pregnant."

"What?" he said, dropping his spoon onto the table with a loud clank. Out of the corner of his eye he saw Mallory turn pale. Oh, no, she was going to faint again. Damn Stella for gossiping. Why hadn't he told her to butt out when she'd appeared at the booth? Didn't it occur to her that the news might hurt Mallory's feelings?

On the other hand, it could be pure hearsay. Diane pregnant? He would have known. She would have been sick a lot in the mornings and thrown up, those things pregnant women did. No, it wasn't possible. So Stella was there to gloat about his misfortune and to show him she knew more than he did about his own ranch and his own foreman. And maybe to make up for the fact she'd lost out on the bidding for a bull he'd bought last year.

She nodded solemnly and ordered a salad and a diet Coke. "That's what I heard. From Randy who heard from Chuck who got it from Joe."

"I wouldn't take anything I heard third-hand very seriously. I would have known if Diane…no, it can't be true. I don't believe it,'' he said firmly with a glance at Mallory who had little worry lines etched between her eyebrows.

"Believe it," she said. "It pays to keep your ear to the grindstone."

"I thought it was your nose."

"Whatever it is, you apparently weren't doing it and now you've lost two of your best workers. If I'd known Joe was leaving, I would have offered him twice what you were paying him. But they say he wanted to get away, put some distance between him and the gossip. How're you ever going to replace him?"

"I already have. Nobody's indispensable, you know."

"We'll see about that. Wait a few weeks and I'll ask you again." She took a sip of her drink and looked across at Mallory. "I don't think I've seen you around. Are you and Zach…"

"Friends," Zach said, before she could open her mouth, "Mallory is an astronomer."

"Really. How fascinating. Could I get some advice from you? I'm a Libra."

Mallory might have smiled at the question if it weren't for the pain in her chest. How many people were gossiping about Joe and the housekeeper? How long would it be before she was part of the gossip? On the other hand, she was grateful to the woman for changing the subject. The best thing she could do now was to play along.

"Libra," Mallory said thoughtfully, gazing off across the crowded restaurant. "Let me see. Yes, now I'm getting it." She shifted her gaze back to Stella. "What you need to do is to stay in your cocoon. Don't stray from home until your moon is in another house. Does this make any sense to you?" she asked.

"Yes, it does. You know I had a feeling I should have

stayed home today. First I had a flat tire and then I broke
my fingernail changing it. Instead of going to the bank,
I'm going right home after lunch. You're amazing, you
know," she said beaming at Mallory. "What's your
sign?" she asked Zach.

"How should I know?" he said.

"When's your birthday?"

"October twenty-eighth."

"You're a Scorpio." Stella turned to Mallory. "What's
in store for him?" she asked.

Mallory surveyed her boss's rugged face as if she knew
what she was doing. "Scorpio," she repeated, her mind
floundering. It didn't help that Zach was looking at her
with an expression brimming with cynicism. "Let's see.
While Mars joins Venus in Capricorn, you should weigh
your options and change direction."

"She's unbelievable, isn't she, Zach?" Stella said,
wide-eyed with wonder.

"Unbelievable is the word for it," he said drily.

"Let's see what the newspaper says," Stella enthused
while Mallory nibbled on her sandwich. "Not that a newspaper would know more than a live astronomer, but
still..." She reached into her bag, pulled out a section of
her newspaper while Mallory nibbled at her sandwich.
"Here we are. Listen to this, Zach. 'Worrisome situations
around home base can be a drag.' Oh, ho, that's definitely
you."

"Pure coincidence," Zach said flatly. "Everyone has
worrisome situations at home base."

"'Your best bet is to act swiftly,'" Stella continued
unabated. "Sounds like you've done that. 'There's a strong
temptation to do something rash. Despite the current chaos,
stay calm. Unexpected good will come of this.'" She tilted
her head to observe his reaction. When there was none,

she continued. "Your thoughts and feelings are at odds," she read loudly. "Since your thoughts are well-known, try siding with your feelings for a change."

He smiled blandly and nudged her arm. "Thank you, Stella, for those words of wisdom. It was good seeing you again." He stood up. Stella had to move so he could get out of the booth. He grabbed Mallory's arm with one hand, the check with the other and almost dragged her along with her shopping bag to the cashier while Stella went back to reading horoscopes.

"The woman doesn't know when to quit. 'Thoughts and feelings at odds.' What garbage," he muttered when they were out on the sidewalk. "What possessed you to play along with her? You didn't have to do that. You could have explained the difference between astrology and astronomy."

"I know, but she didn't want to hear that. She wanted someone to tell her what to do. So I did."

"Am I the only one who doesn't want to hear my horoscope? Tex believes in the stars, too." He was irritated by this run-in with Stella, but he was grateful for one thing. His horoscope mentioned nothing about romance. Not that he believed in that kind of thing.

He led Mallory down the Creek Walk that wound through the downtown to get back to his truck, his hand clamped on her elbow. As if he was afraid she was going to run away. He had another housekeeper, so why should he care if she ran? He didn't know why, but he did care.

"Sorry you had to hear all that garbage about Joe. I don't know how these rumors get started."

Mallory paused at the edge of the creek to set her shopping bag down and catch her breath. She was still shaking after hearing what the woman said about Joe. She wished she'd never come to town. It certainly made hiding out at the ranch more desirable, at least until the gossip died down.

"Then you don't believe…what she said?" she asked, glancing up at him.

"Of course not. It's not possible. I would have noticed if Diane…no, no way."

She straightened. "Wait a minute. You don't even know what Diane wore or even if she was pretty. So how would you have known if she was pregnant?" She told herself it didn't matter if it was true or not. Joe was gone and out of her life. She was on her own. She had a new job and she was going to do it the best she could. She smoothed the fabric of her new striped shirt that hung over matching blue shorts. If it wasn't what a housekeeper wore, she was sorry. It was comfortable and it was what she was going to wear.

Zach didn't answer. He was watching a small boy throw stones across the water. She didn't expect him to answer. What could he say? Not only did he know nothing about love, he obviously knew nothing about women.

She leaned against the fence that bordered the creek and gazed off at the rippling water of the creek.

Zach stood next to her. "Reminds me of me," he said, pointing to the boy. "Skipping stones across our stream."

"Must have been a nice place to grow up," she said, grateful for the change of subject. "Did you say your uncle raised you?"

"If you can call it that. He was more into raising cattle than kids. He didn't know what to do with me, so he didn't do anything." His voice was matter-of-fact, and held not a trace of self pity.

"How did you learn about ranching?" she asked, slanting a glance at his rugged profile.

"From the crew, the foreman, anybody who'd take the time to show me what they were doing."

"Weren't you lonely?" she asked, resting her chin on the top of the fence.

"I don't know. I spent a lot of time by myself, I know that much. Riding. Thinking. Throwing stones. Sometimes I hung out in the bunkhouse. I'd sit in the corner where they wouldn't notice me. The guys used to sit around after dinner and tell stories, or somebody would play the harmonica. It was nice. Better than being in the big empty house with Uncle Walt."

"I take it he wasn't a lot of fun."

"His idea of fun was getting a good price for his cattle."

"What's your idea of fun?" Mallory asked.

"Don't you ever get tired of asking questions?" he asked brusquely, the reminiscing clearly over. He picked up her bag for her. "Let's go."

She nodded. As she tried to keep up with his long-legged stride down the path, she couldn't help thinking of a small boy in the corner of the bunkhouse where no one could see him. Where no one knew he was there. Where he smiled at the cowboys' banter and listened to their music.

She could see him now. A little boy with dark hair and blue, blue eyes. A small lonely boy whose mother had "dumped" him and whose father had deserted him. A boy who'd grown into a man without ever knowing he was lonely. Maybe that explained his brusque manner, his disclaimer on love, his determination not to feel sorry for himself or accept sympathy for the losses in his life. Her heart twisted. Maybe he didn't want her sympathy, but it welled up inside her and threatened to spill over. She wanted to reach for his hand and squeeze it. To tell him she understood.

Instead he reached for her hand. Her heart gave a jolt. Until she realized the gesture had nothing to do with sympathy or feelings. It was just to pull her along. To speed up the process. The better to drag her all over town while he did his errands, stopping at the saddlery and buying a new pair of boots. By the time he'd finished, it was late afternoon. She was tired, let-down and she still didn't know what a housekeeper did.

"I'm afraid we've missed dinner," he said as they drove down the highway toward the ranch. Shadows were lengthening across the alfalfa fields on either side of the road. "But Tex will put something aside for us."

"He's a wonderful cook. I thought maybe the housekeeper had to—"

"No. I told you, the housekeeper's job is to supervise. Naturally the housekeeper *can* cook."

"Naturally," she murmured. She didn't know why the housekeeper had to be able to cook, if there already was a cook. She could cook. A little. But a crew of ravenous cowboys ate a lot of hearty food. Thank heavens for Tex. If everyone knew their job as well as Tex did, then what was there to supervise?

"But how will Tex feel about being supervised by an out-of-work astronomer?" she asked.

"It won't bother him a bit," Zach assured her. "He's taken a liking to you."

"That's nice," she said. "But once he finds out my only useful skill around the place is to give dubious advice based on the position of the stars, then what?"

"Then nothing. I'm telling you not to worry. You'll grow into the job."

She sighed. If he only knew how much she was really going to grow.

She leaned her head back against the headrest. Maybe

that was the answer. Let them think astronomers received information from the stars. She'd give advice when people asked. Just like she'd done for Stella. That's what they wanted. They didn't want to be supervised. They just wanted to do their job and they wanted to hear what the stars had in store for them. They wanted to know what to do. She couldn't blame them. She wanted to know what to do, too.

Three

Zach was right. Tex had left food for them in the refrigerator. He went directly to the kitchen, while Mallory went to her room. He heated two plates of meat loaf, mashed potatoes and green beans in the microwave oven and waited for her, but she never came. Finally he ate without her, angry with himself for worrying whether she ate or not. She was a grown-up, twenty-eight years old, and if she didn't want her dinner, that was her problem.

But instead of going to his office after dinner as he usually did, he went to her room. Not to see if she was all right, but to tell her about the new housekeeper. It wasn't fair to lead her on or keep her in the dark. She might want to make plans. She definitely should make plans.

So he headed down the hall before he could chicken out. These things didn't usually bother him. Over the years he'd probably fired a couple dozen men. It was a given. Wranglers didn't stay long in one place. But housekeepers, they were another matter. And astronomers? He suspected they drifted from one observatory to another. She was probably used to it.

He knocked on her door. No answer. He pushed the door open. The scent of hothouse flowers wafted out. How fast the room had changed. Her things on the desk. Her clothes in the closet. Her perfume in the air. He'd given her a key, but she hadn't locked the door. She was too trusting. Too naïve. Leaving her door unlocked. Falling for the most notorious ladies' man in the whole county. God only knew what she'd do next.

He walked outside, lit a cigar and took the trail to the hill overlooking the lake. He wouldn't admit that he was relieved she wasn't around so he couldn't fire her. He'd never admit he was worried about where she was. Good thing he *hadn't* wasted time worrying about where she was, because she was there, at the top of the hill, sitting on a collapsible camp stool, peering through her telescope. He crushed his cigar under his heel, but the smell of the smoke had already announced his arrival. She turned to watch him walk toward her through the dark field of poppies, closed tight until morning.

"How're things with the nebulae?" he asked.

"It's incredible," she enthused. "I've never been able to see an interstellar cloud before. They're too cold, you understand, to emit any light."

"I understand," he said.

"But a cold cloud can absorb the light from bright objects like stars behind it. Then it's silhouetted against the background light." Her voice rose, bright with excitement. "Here, take a look." She got up off the stool and motioned him to take her place.

He pressed one eye shut and looked through the telescope with the other. All he saw was a blurry mass.

She stood behind him, her hands resting lightly on his shoulders. "What do you see?" she asked impatiently.

"Not much," he admitted. Good thing she didn't ask what he felt. He didn't want her to know that her touch, however light, however innocent, sent a shaft of desire rocketing through him like a comet. He wanted to lean back, and cushion his head in the apex of her thighs. He wanted her attention to shift from the stars to himself. He was jealous of the stars! He was an idiot. Resolutely he kept his eye pressed to the lens.

"Really? Let me see what's wrong." She reached around him to change the angle of the telescope. Her breasts pressed into his back. Her arms were wrapped around his. If he turned his head her cheek would brush against his. He clenched his teeth and told himself this wasn't the time or the place. There *was* no time and no place. Not for them. She'd just been jilted, and he wasn't interested in taking up where Joe left off.

"Okay," she said. "Try again."

He pressed his eye to the glass. "Still a blur," he said.

"I know," she said, "I'll adjust the lens so you can see something more familiar, more spectacular."

It took her a long time. It took her forever. She turned the knob, loosened the clamp and rotated the stand. Then turned the knob again. And all the while he sat there, subjected to the subtle adjustments she made in her telescope and the not-so-subtle adjustments of her body against his. Her hands brushed his, her breasts grazed his back, her cheek collided with his as she checked the view over and over again.

And the scent, the overwhelming, tantalizing smell of her hair and her skin. Another minute and he'd explode. One more time that her hair brushed against his temple and he'd be forced to do something rash, despite the warning of his horoscope. Of course he could have stood, let her have the stool and gotten out of her way. But he didn't.

"Spectacular, like what?" he asked, his voice sounding hoarse in his ears. He couldn't imagine seeing anything more spectacular than her by moonlight.

"Saturn." With her hands on the back of his head, she guided his head back down to the eyepiece. "Isn't it beautiful? Do you see its rings? They're made of tiny particles, each one orbiting the planet."

"Amazing," he said. He wanted to prolong the moment. The moment when the wind in the trees died to a whisper, and the touch of her hands made him feel like he might zoom into orbit himself. "What about Venus?" he asked. "Is it really joining Mars in Capricorn?"

She laughed softly. A sound like rustling leaves. A sound that made his heart pound. He realized he had the power to make her laugh. It was an intoxicating feeling. It made him want to stay there all night looking at the sky with her arms around him.

"I'm afraid you're too late for Venus," she said. "Tomorrow if you come out earlier you can see it. You won't even need my telescope."

"I'll need you to point it out to me."

She shook her head. "I don't think so. It'll be the brightest thing in the western sky. And it won't be in Capricorn. I made that up."

He raised his head. "You didn't," he said.

She nodded and moved away to sit on the grass, hug her knees to her chest and tilt her head back.

"In case you're wondering, that's just a rumor about women being from Venus," she said. "Somebody else made that up. It's actually too hot up there for us. Hot enough to melt lead."

"What about men being from Mars?" he asked, casually dropping to the grass next to her.

"I don't know. There may have been life on Mars at one time. Primitive life, of course. So it's possible. Yes, quite possible," she said thoughtfully.

He lay flat on his back. "Hey, there's the Big Dipper."

"And Orion the Hunter and the Pleiades," she said.

Her enthusiasm was contagious. He edged away from her. He didn't want to catch anything from her, especially not enthusiasm. He might never recover.

"You're so lucky, you know," she continued. "To see this clearly without even binoculars. If you were in the city…"

"I couldn't live in the city."

"You've lived here most all your life, since you were ten, right?"

"Right. That's when my mother dropped me off."

"That's so sad," she said.

"Not at all. Nobody to tell me what to do. I didn't mind."

"Is that the way you'd raise your kids, without any supervision?"

"I'm not going to have kids," he said leaning back on his elbows, "so it's not an issue."

"Why not?" she asked.

He shrugged. "I've got cows to raise. And a ranch to run. No time for kids. Just like my uncle. Besides, in case you haven't noticed, I'm not married and have no intention of getting married again. Once was enough for me. More than enough. Not that being single stops some people from having kids," he said thinking of the gossip he'd heard over lunch.

"Who do you mean?" she asked, her voice tinged with anxiety.

"Oh come on. You haven't lived in a cave these past twenty years. It's not just movie stars. Ordinary people have kids without the benefit of marriage."

"Oh, you're speaking generally."

"I'm speaking specifically. My dad never married my mother. I never knew him. I don't understand that mentality. Father a child and then not stick around to face the music. Left my mother in a bind. Lucky for her and for me there was my uncle."

"Yes."

He glanced at her profile silhouetted in the dark. Her dark hair was gilded by the moonlight. The ripe curves of her body were camouflaged by an oversize flannel shirt and baggy blue jeans. But he remembered them only too well. How they felt pressed against his body. How she looked over the dinner table. Delectable in baggy pants. Desirable in shorts or snug shirts. Even more so by moonlight.

"Been up here long?" he asked.

"Yes, I couldn't wait to set up my telescope."

"You didn't have dinner," he stated.

"I wasn't hungry."

He stood up. "Are you almost finished here? I'll carry your telescope back."

"I can manage." She covered the lens with a cap and folded her tripod.

"I insist," he said lifting the telescope and resting it on his shoulder. "I need to talk to you about something," he said.

"Really? I need to talk to you, too."

She was going to tell him she was quitting. He knew it. He felt it in his bones. He was relieved. He wouldn't have to tell her she was fired. On the other hand, he wasn't relieved. He was angry. She couldn't quit. She'd given her word.

They walked in silence down the hill toward the house. Each one preparing their speech.

This isn't easy to say... It's only fair to tell you...

He flipped the light switch in the kitchen. The copper pots hanging from the rack on the ceiling glowed. The smell of cinnamon wafted from the yeast rolls rising on the countertop.

Her stomach growled.

"Hungry?" he asked.

"Yes."

He opened the refrigerator. "There's meat loaf."

"No thanks."

"You didn't eat your beef last night. Are you a vegetarian?"

"No, at least I never was before. But now, I don't know why, I can't eat it. I could eat an omelet though. With mushrooms and cheese and spinach." Her mouth watered. She wanted an omelet. She craved an omelet. She had to have one. Even if she had to drive to town to get it.

He shot her a curious look, but he didn't say anything. From the depths of the refrigerator he came up with three eggs, a chunk of cheddar cheese and a box of mushrooms.

"Everything but the spinach. And the kitchen sink."

"Thank you."

Mallory beat eggs, she grated cheese and she sliced mushrooms, while he sat with his stocking feet propped on the small pine breakfast table and watched. Whenever she looked up he was still looking at her, a strange and intense look in those deep blue eyes. As if he could see right into her soul. Or even worse, right into her body. She wondered what he was thinking. Wondered if he could possibly guess.

She dropped a lump of butter in the cast-iron pan. Tucked a strand of hair behind her ear. Her face was flushed from the heat of the gas flames. In a few minutes it was done. Brown on the outside and creamy on the inside. She slid it on a plate. He lowered his feet to the floor and went to the refrigerator.

"Want some of this?" she asked, holding out her plate.

He shook his head and cut himself a slice of cold meat loaf. Then he sat across from her at the small pine kitchen table, eating his meat loaf while she stuffed herself with the huge, delicious omelet. The best thing she'd eaten in weeks. She felt his eyes on her, his benign, almost amused glances. She didn't care if he thought she was a pig. She was hungry.

"There," she said at last as she washed it all down with a swallow of cold milk. "Now, what was it you had to tell me?"

"You go first," he said.

"No you," she said.

"I insist."

"All right. Maybe you already know this, but one of your ranch hands, Marv, I think his name is, found your lost cows."

His mouth fell open in surprise. "The mavericks? How do you know?"

"I saw him on my way up the hill. One of your neighbors called, and this Marv went to get them. He said he'd left a note for you."

"I didn't get it. But that's good news."

"Now it's your turn."

"I was going to say that I found a foreman, but you already know that."

"Yes. Tell me, aren't you afraid I'll run off with him?"

He grinned. She was shocked. She'd never even seen him smile before. Didn't know if he did. If he could. The grin lit up his face. Made him look years younger. Handsome. She wanted to freeze-frame the moment. In case it never happened again.

"What's so funny?" she asked.

"He's about ninety years old."

"How do you know I don't have a thing for older men?" she asked with a flirtatious smile playing at the corners of her mouth.

"Do you?" he asked, his eyebrows drawn together in a frown.

"Depends. There are older men and there are *older men*."

"And I thought you were naïve."

"I was." She sighed. And ran her finger around the rim of her glass. "I'm not anymore. I have something else to tell you."

He stood up. "Save it for tomorrow."

As he passed her chair, she held out her hand without thinking. He caught her by the wrist and jerked her out of her seat to face him. He was so close she could feel his heat. Smell the grass he'd been sitting on and the musky male scent that invaded her senses. She knew how it would feel if he kissed her. First the scrape of the coarse shadow of a beard that lined his jaw against her tender skin. Then his mouth on hers. Joining her in deep, urgent kisses. Hot, soulful kisses to remind her she was not a castoff, she was a desirable woman. The kitchen was warm, so warm her face flamed.

Somewhere deep inside her a burning knot of desire grew and threatened to burst into fire. It wouldn't take much to set it off. Just a small match. With his one hand still holding hers, and the other at the small of her back, he pulled her close, so close she could feel his arousal press against her belly.

This couldn't be happening. Not with someone she

barely knew. Hadn't she learned her lesson yet? She felt
her chest heaving as she tried to suck in enough air to
speak.

"I have to tell you now," she insisted. "I have to tell
somebody."

Four

There was a long moment of silence. During which she tried again to speak but couldn't. The words stuck in her throat.

"Boss?" It was Tex, in flannel pajamas, blinking sleepily in the doorway. "I thought I heard something. Want something to eat?"

"No thanks, Tex," Zach said in a rough voice, releasing her reluctantly.

"Hello there, Ms. Mallory. Didn't see you for a moment."

"Hi, Tex." She was proud of how steady her voice was. Not so proud of stalling, of not telling Zach what she had to tell him while she'd had a chance.

"Seen your horoscope yet today?" he asked her.

"Why no, I haven't."

Tex picked up a newspaper from a stack under the sink. "Then I'll read it to you," he said. "What's your sign?"

She shot a puzzled look at Zach. He shrugged and leaned back against the tiles. She sat down again.

"Aquarius," she said.

Tex nodded, and began to read. "'Those who tend to write you off as just a pretty face are dead wrong. You have clear goals and would like to get cracking on them. This week, however, you'll have a hard time just keeping your head when no one around you seems to have one. Be patient just a little longer.'" He glanced up at her with a perplexed frown. "That make sense to you?"

"Sort of," she said, looking longingly in the direction of the door to the hallway. She was exhausted. No nap today, she reminded herself. No wonder she was tired. It had been a long day. A day of fending off speculation, of second-guessing her employer and now her horoscope telling her to be patient. She sighed impatiently.

"She does have a pretty face, though. Don't you think so?" he asked Zach.

"Very pretty," Zach said rubbing his hand across his face.

What else could he say, Mallory wondered, with her in the same room? "Thanks, Tex," she said heading for the door. "Good night everyone." She trudged down the hall wondering if every night ended like this around here, with the boss and the cook engaged in late-night conversation. Maybe it was a carryover from the days when Zach was young and hung out with the ranch hands in the bunkhouse. Maybe the company of his workers made up for the lack of a family. There was something about a big, homey kitchen with yeast rolls rising on the range that made her think of her grandma's kitchen, the only real home she'd ever had.

Clear goals, she thought, thinking of her horoscope, as

she dug her granny gown out from the bottom of her drawer. What were they? She got into bed and began counting. To get her research done. Which didn't include giving beginning astronomy lessons to her employer. To get through the summer without losing her head. To avoid any further disastrous entanglements like the one that got her into her present predicament.

And last but not least, tell him. Quit stalling. She promised herself she'd tell him the next day. Then she ticked off a few more goals like keeping her relationship with her employer on a professional level, still wondering what would have happened if Tex hadn't come into the kitchen when he did. Be patient, her horoscope said. Easy for them to say. Good general advice for anyone and everyone. But what did that mean to her? she wondered. Nothing, she told herself as she drifted off.

There was nothing patient about the ringing of the doorbell the next morning. Mallory, her appetite returned with a vengeance, had just finished a breakfast of pancakes and hot chocolate and was on her way to the laundry in her continuing effort to figure out what a housekeeper was supposed to do.

Answering the door was certainly one of the things, she supposed, opening the door to a short, chubby woman in a bright blue suit and a straw hat perched on curly iron gray hair. She was carrying a small suitcase in one hand.

"Mr. Calhoun here?" she asked.

"I'll see," Mallory said. "Does he expect you?"

"Sure does. I'm Cass Bloomberg. Heard he was desperate for a housekeeper. Came as fast as I could."

"Oh, no, he's already found one. I'm afraid you're just a few days late," Mallory said with a polite smile.

"But I just heard yesterday. Yesterday was when Mr.

Calhoun came into the employment office. That's what Frank said. Said Mr. Calhoun needed a foreman and a housekeeper right away. On account of what happened. You know.''

Mallory stiffened. "You're sure it was yesterday."

"Yes, ma'am."

"I'll tell him you're here," Mallory said, turning on her heel and stomping down the hall toward the office. Her eyes burned, anger surged through her veins. So that's what he'd wanted to tell her. That she was fired. Only one day after she was hired. No wonder he couldn't bring himself to do it. He'd had all morning, then lunchtime, and all afternoon while she'd followed him around town, then all the way home and all evening on the hill and still later in the kitchen. And still he didn't tell her. Joe didn't tell her he couldn't marry her, and Zach didn't tell her he couldn't hire her. What was wrong with men, anyway?

She flung open the door to the richly appointed office to find Zach consulting with his accountant at one end of the long oval table. They were both smoking cigars, and the air was blue with smoke. They looked up simultaneously as she stood in the doorway seething with anger.

"How dare you," she began, her voice shaking uncontrollably.

Zach pushed his chair from the table. "Would you excuse us, Jay?"

The accountant grabbed a handful of papers, stuffed them in his briefcase, rushed past Mallory and out the door. He closed it firmly behind him.

Zach put his hands on her shoulders and eased Mallory into the nearest chair. "Calm down. Take a deep breath. How dare I what?"

"How dare you hire another housekeeper? When were you going to tell me? When were you going to fire me?"

"Oh, Lord." Zach raked his hand through his hair. "I forgot all about her. When? I don't know. I tell you I forgot about her. And I'm not going to fire you."

"Then why…" Plumes of smoke from the forgotten cigars in the ashtray wafted her way. Her stomach revolted. "The bathroom," she muttered, getting to her feet.

He opened the door to the adjoining bathroom, and she staggered in as if she'd been on an all-night bender.

When she came out he'd ground out the cigars, opened the windows and was standing at the table, his hands braced on the back of her chair, a fathomless look in his blue eyes.

"You okay?" he asked.

The way he was observing her pale face, he had to know she wasn't. At the very least she was suffering from extreme humiliation and an advanced case of embarrassment.

"Fine," she lied, sliding into her chair again.

He sat down next to her at the large boardroom table. She felt his gaze on her, tracing the outline of her body with his eyes. "You're pregnant, aren't you?" he said at last.

She swallowed hard, fighting to keep the tears down and nodded. "I tried to tell you."

"Not very hard," he observed drily.

"I'm sorry, but at least you've got your housekeeper. She's in the foyer. She was, anyway."

"She'll wait." His eyes narrowed. "Joe's baby?"

"Yes."

"So that's why you were going to marry him," Zach said. "And that's why he left. The bastard."

"It's not entirely his fault," she said burying her burning face in her hands so she wouldn't have to look at him. "He didn't force me to do anything I didn't want to do."

"He could have married you."

"He said he would and I think he intended to. But..." Tears threatened. She choked them back. "Fatherhood's a scary business."

"What about motherhood?" he asked.

She gave him a wry, watery smile and nodded. "Uh-huh."

"What now?" he asked her, standing and pacing back and forth in front of the open windows.

"I don't know," she said. "But don't worry about me, I'll—"

"Don't *worry*? Don't worry about you? You arrive here with all your worldly goods, faint in my living room, move into my house, throw up in my bathroom and then you tell me not to worry about you?" Angry sparks shot out of his eyes. "What do you expect me to do?" he demanded.

"I expect you to throw me out," she said simply.

"That's what you think of me?" he asked incredulously. "My God, what kind of men are you used to?" He pounded his fist on the table. "Don't tell me. It's men like Joe. How many have there been? No, don't tell me, I don't want to know. Don't you have anything to say?" he demanded.

"If you'd give me a chance," she said, gripping the edge of her chair.

He pressed his lips together and swept his arm in a wide gesture indicating she should go ahead.

She took a deep breath. "There haven't been any others. That's why... That's why I don't know what to do."

"Want my advice?" he asked.

"I have a feeling you're going to give it to me whether I want it or not," she said.

"Stay here. Stay right where you are. In Diane's room."

"What about Mrs...."

"We'll find a place for her. There's an apartment over

the garage. It might be vacant. Diane would know. But Diane, well—you know.''

Mallory stifled the urge to scream. If she never heard anyone mention the name Diane again it would be too soon for her.

''I can't just live here,'' she protested. ''I've got to—''

''Work, I know. Because of your Puritan upbringing. There's plenty of work around here. You can be the house-keeper's assistant. But no physical work. No lifting, no bending.''

Mallory gasped with surprise. ''How do you know what I can do and what I can't? How do you know anything about pregnant women?''

''I know about pregnant shorthorns.''

''I suppose they're not allowed to lift, either.''

''Damn right. If I catch them so much as eyeing a big heavy bale of hay I confine them to a stall until they calve.''

''I'd hate to be confined to a stall for the next five months,'' she murmured.

''Then follow my orders.''

She lifted her hand to her forehead to give him a mock salute. The man was a dictator. A benevolent dictator, but a dictator all the same. Then she paused. She was still uncertain. Still full of doubts about how this strange ar-rangement would work. ''Are you sure I'll have something to do? Because I won't be a charity case. I do have other options.''

Fortunately he didn't ask what they were, because she couldn't think of a single one at that point.

''Five months?'' he said, his eyes lingering on the slight swell of her stomach and moving up to rest on her full breasts. Just his gaze alone set off a heat wave in her body. Made her breasts tingle as if he'd touched them and started a melting sensation in the core of her body. Her backbone collapsed and she slid down in her chair.

In the midst of these disturbing sensations, she realized that Zach had sounded surprised when she'd said five months. She'd caught him off guard. He didn't want her there that long.

She twisted her fingers together. "That's a long time," she said. "Maybe I'd better—"

"Maybe you'd better see a doctor next time we go to town."

"We?"

"I'm going with you. I want to make sure everything's okay."

She pulled herself up straight in the chair. "I saw the doctor last month. Everything *is* okay. Besides you're not responsible for me."

"Joe got you pregnant. Joe was my foreman. Joe's gone. Therefore I'm responsible."

She sighed loudly. But she didn't protest. She was annoyed by his overprotective manner, yet she was oddly touched. Here was a man who knew nothing about women, who'd never been in love and never even known love, and yet he was concerned about her welfare. Talk about the Puritan work ethic. The man had a giant Puritan sense of responsibility.

"Speaking of responsibility," Mallory said. "Shouldn't you do something about Mrs. Bloomberg. If she's still there?"

She thought he'd forgotten about her. She imagined he would slap his palm against his forehead and leap to his feet. But he didn't.

"Right," he said, and calmly stood up and walked out. He looked preoccupied, as if his mind was somewhere else and not on his new housekeeper.

Five

"**I**'ve never worked where there wasn't a woman in charge," Cass Bloomberg said after she'd recited her work history and handed Zach an envelope full of hand-written recommendations. He leafed through them, certain he was going to hire her unless she had a prison record, then made her an offer she couldn't refuse. A generous salary and an apartment over the garage.

Zach leaned against the mantel of the fireplace in the living room and observed his new housekeeper who was in turn observing him over a pair of granny glasses.

"I mean usually there's a wife, or someone who runs the house," she said.

"This ranch has always been run by a man, for better or worse. First my uncle and then me. That's the way it is."

"And who, may I ask, was the woman who answered the door?"

"That was Mallory, your assistant."

She frowned. "I don't need an assistant. Never had one before."

"There's a first for everything. This is a big ranch."

"I've worked at big ranches before. The Binghams' for example. I reported directly to Mrs. Bingham. And I never had an assistant there."

"Well, you've got one now."

"I suppose I do. What is she supposed to do, besides answer the door?"

"A little of everything. She's very good at what she does. But no lifting. Nothing strenuous," Zach said firmly.

"Why, does she have back trouble?"

"Something like that. You'll want to see your apartment. I'll get somebody to show it to you." He left Cass Bloomberg there on the couch and went back to the office where he found Mallory still in her chair. She was staring dreamily out the open window at the sun-dappled meadows in the distance with a faraway look in her eyes.

"What's wrong?" he asked.

She jumped up with a guilty start. "Nothing. I was just thinking...just looking at the view. Admiring the wildflowers. They're gorgeous. They smell good too. What happened?"

"I hired her. She seems competent."

"What did you tell her about me?"

"That you're her assistant. She's never had one before. So she doesn't quite know what to do with you."

"Welcome to the club," Mallory murmured. "You didn't say anything about...about..."

"No."

"One of these days I'm going to have to tell people."

He looked down at her with narrowed eyes, following the contours of her body with his gaze, the outline of her breasts and her hips until his heart was thundering so loud he was afraid she'd hear it. What was wrong with him, lusting after a woman pregnant with someone else's child?

He forced his eyes upward to meet her troubled gaze. So far her pregnancy was her secret. *Their* secret. But she was right, she would have to tell someone before long. Telling someone would mean everyone would know. How long would it be before that happened? He didn't want everyone to know. Hated the gossip that would surface. A fierce sense of protection surged through his veins. He had a crazy wish to keep her locked away until the baby came. He shrugged it off as some misguided sense of propriety.

"I suppose you will have to tell people eventually," he said, his voice carefully neutral. "About Cass, you'll work it out between you what you'll do. Now to find her a place to stay. If you're feeling better, could you check the apartment over the garage? If it's empty, have Juana clean it. If it's not—"

"I'll find something else."

Zach heaved a sigh of relief. "Good girl."

"No problem."

"And while you're at it, could you find housing for the new foreman? I expect him any minute now. There's got to be a master housing list somewhere. I need to finish up with Jay, my accountant, the one I was talking to—"

"When I burst in on you. I'm sorry about that. I don't usually throw temper tantrums."

"Good, because that's my next order. No lifting, no throwing."

Mallory sighed. "Not even a tantrum."

"Especially not a tantrum. Stress is bad for the baby."

Mallory rolled her eyes. "I suppose you know that because of your experience with cows?"

"You got it. You see those cattle out there? Half of

them are calving this year. Do they look worried? Do they look stressed? Are they going to produce the best calves in this whole state? The answers are no, no and yes.'' His heart filled with pride at the sight of his placid cows in the distance, peacefully munching on the rich summer grasses.

''All right,'' she agreed, gazing out at the pastoral scene. ''I'll try to stay calm.''

''Do that,'' he said.

She nodded and walked past him and out the door, leaving a faint trail of her perfume mingled with lavender soap behind to tantalize him. Not for the first time he wondered what in the hell he was doing, hiring three new people in two days. One overbearing, opinionated housekeeper, an aged but experienced foreman and an assistant housekeeper without a clue as to what to do, but who tempted him like a ripe summer fruit bursting with flavor. A forbidden fruit he could only look at and not taste.

He ticked off the reasons why she was off limits to him:

She worked for him.

She'd been Joe's girl. For one night, anyway.

She was pregnant.

She would leave. Just like every other woman in his life. After the baby came, she'd be gone.

Why had he hired her? It didn't matter if it was pity, his overgrown sense of responsibility or that fierce, protective feeling that came over him when he picked her up off the floor—the same feeling that hit him when he realized she was pregnant. Whatever it was, she was there. For the next five months, anyway. In his house, in his thoughts and in his dreams.

Yes, he'd dreamed about her last night. Dreamed of lying with her under the stars. Or maybe it was the nebulae. Whatever it was, she was there with him, her head on his shoulder, her hair brushing his cheek, her hip pressed against his, her long legs—

"Are you free now?" The accountant stood in the doorway, his briefcase still in hand.

"Come on in, Jay," Zach said, reluctantly jerked back to the real world. "Let's get this over with." Because as soon as he got it over with, he had to go over to the bunkhouse and talk to the crew, call a man about a new bull and of course check up on his new housekeeper. And her assistant.

"My previous bosses were all women," Cass said to Mallory as she handed her a bedsheet in the studio apartment above the garage. "I thought there'd be a Mrs. Calhoun,"

"I believe there was at one time," Mallory said cautiously.

"What happened to her?"

"She left. But that was a long time ago. Before my time," Mallory said. She wished she didn't have to participate in this gossip mill. She wished even more that she wouldn't be the object of such gossip. But it was inevitable. As soon as people found out about her condition.

"Then he's not taken?" Cass asked. "He's available now?"

Mallory gripped one edge of the flowered sheet while Cass held the other edge and together they smoothed it over the queen-size bed. Next came a blue blanket. And after that a comforter. After that Mallory finally answered the question.

"He's not taken, no. But he's not available, either," Mallory said. It was hard to understand, she thought noting the confusion in the older woman's eyes, but that's the way it was. "I don't believe he's interested in getting involved with a woman again.'' Mallory bit her tongue. Why did she have to share that bit of information? It was none of her business and it was none of Cass's business. ''Actually,'' Mallory continued lamely, ''I'm new here myself so I don't know too much about him.''

''Sounds like there's quite a rapid turnover.''

''Not really,'' Mallory said. ''Some of the people have been here for years. Take the cook for example.''

''I haven't met him yet. You mean he's not already taken, either?''

''Well I don't know. What I meant was...''

''I know what you meant, dear. You run along now. I can manage the rest. As I told Mr. Calhoun I'm not used to having an assistant. I never had one at the Bingham Ranch. It seems odd that he'd hire an assistant before hiring a housekeeper.'' The older woman crossed her arms over her ample waist.

Mallory nodded in agreement. Odd was putting it mildly. Mallory hoped Cass wouldn't find out just *how* odd the situation was. But she probably would, it was just a matter of time.

''Although Mr. Calhoun says you're very good at what you do.''

''Does he?'' Mallory asked, curious about what else he'd said about her.

''Here's what we'll do,'' Cass said. ''Starting tomorrow, we'll divide up the work, then we won't get in each other's way. You stick to the big house, since you live there, with the kitchen and so forth and I'll do the actual housekeeping, that is the cleaning and upkeep of the cabins and such.'' She waved her hand toward the window and the cluster of cottages on the hill.

''All right,'' Mallory said, faintly relieved. ''But Zach, Mr. Calhoun that is, asked me to place you and the new foreman in housing. As soon as I find a place for him, the job is all yours. There is a maid, by the way, several maids, I think. So you don't actually have to do any cleaning. Just supervising," Mallory said, as if she knew what she was talking about. Here she was explaining her job to a real, experienced housekeeper.

"Huh! I've never met a maid who did a thorough enough job. Girls these days don't know anything about elbow grease. I always come along after them and get down on my hands and knees with a scrub brush. But with your back problem I suppose you'll have to rely on me or on the maids for the hard work."

"My back problem?"

"What is it, a slipped disk?" Cass asked.

"No. No it isn't." Puzzled, Mallory smoothed the pillow. "Now, would you like a tour of the property?"

"Does it involve any walking?"

"Well..."

"At the Bingham Ranch, where I used to work, they had a golf cart to get around."

"How handy. But I thought on a ranch everyone rode a horse."

Cass snorted. "Not this lady."

"Well, let me see what I can do," Mallory said.

"And while you're at it, I'll need a list of employees, where they live, a map of the property, a list of suppliers and a list of the single men."

"What?"

"There's bound to be someone in my age bracket on a ranch of this size," Cass said. "And it's best to approach these things methodically. At my age I can't afford to leave anything to chance. Tell me about this new foreman."

"I understand he's a mature man." Certainly ninety could be considered mature.

"Really?" Cass glanced at her reflection in the mirror on top of the dresser and patted her gray curls. "Does he play bridge?"

Mallory said she didn't know, then slipped away, promising to do her best to supply the housekeeper with the items she'd requested. Including a golf cart and a man in her age bracket. Cass had a self-confidence she admired. A way of giving orders that wasn't offensive but brooked no insubordination. A certain can-do, no-nonsense attitude she herself would do well to emulate.

But first she had to find a place for the new foreman. Didn't it make sense to give him the former foreman's house? Mallory set off for Joe's cabin, walking around the weathered redwood barn to the path. Was it only two days ago she'd walked this way with Zach? The day she'd learned she wouldn't be getting married after all. The day she'd fainted in Zach's living room.

Even while out cold on his floor she'd been conscious of him picking her up and carrying her across the room. Aware, at some level of her being, of his strength and his power. And a gentleness he would never admit. As she passed the barn door she heard voices. One belonged to her boss. Curious, she stopped in her tracks and listened shamelessly to the conversation.

"...should be arriving today and he'll know what special feed to order."

"Didn't take you long to replace Joe or Diane either. That Mallory is one good-looking housekeeper."

"Assistant housekeeper. Don't get any ideas, Perry."

"Why not, is she taken?"

Mallory pressed her ear against the rough board, but she couldn't hear his response. What did he say?

"....not a real housekeeper," Zach said.

"What is she?" Perry asked.

A horse whinnied and Mallory missed the answer. She wished she'd heard it, because she wanted to know too. Was she an out-of-work astronomer, an assistant housekeeper who didn't know how to housekeep? Or was she a pregnant single mother-to-be with raging hormones? At that moment the double doors swung open and Perry and Zach came out leading a proud-looking sorrel mare.

"Here she is now," Perry said, greeting her with a big smile. "What does an assistant housekeeper do, anyway?"

Mallory took a deep breath, then took a clue from Cass and squared her shoulders. "She oversees the kitchen and the main house," she said briskly in her best imitation of the new housekeeper. "And for today only, since Cass just arrived, the assistant housekeeper finds housing for the new employees. Perry, I know you were interested in Joe's cabin, but I'm going to have to assign it to the new foreman." She stared unblinking into his eyes. And waited for his protest.

"You can't do that. We had a deal. I deserve that place, I should have it. I've been here longer than anybody. My place isn't big enough and the carpet's worn out. Tell her, Zach."

Zach shook his head. "This is a housekeeping decision. You know I never interfere in internal affairs."

"That cabin traditionally belongs to the foreman," Mallory said firmly, hoping no one would contradict her. "But you can ask Cass about the carpet. She seems very efficient and she's had lots of experience."

Perry sighed loudly but finally agreed to approach the new housekeeper.

"I know you've been here a long time, but Slim is older than you, Perry, and he is the foreman," Mallory added.

"Older than me?" Perry said. "I didn't know anybody was older than me. Okay, okay, so I'll stay where I am.

Just when I was making plans to invite you down to my new cabin to see my etchings,'' he said with a wink, his disappointment forgotten.

She chuckled at his blatant flirtatiousness, and out of the corner of her eye she saw Zach stiffen. Perry grinned. ''What's wrong, boss? You said she wasn't taken.''

''There's a new rule. Starting today, no fraternizing among employees. That way no one runs away with anyone.''

''Does that include you?'' Perry asked Zach.

''Don't you have work to do, Perry?'' Zach asked pointedly. ''I thought you were going to the south forty this morning.''

''I clean forgot. Got so interested in our conversation with Ms. Mallory here. See y'all at lunch.'' He swung up on the horse and tipped his hat to Mallory before he rode off.

Zach leaned against the barn door. ''I hope the new rule won't cramp your style,'' he said, letting his gaze wander over her stretch jeans and her extra-long knit shirt. It annoyed him to hear her banter with Perry. It wasn't that he was jealous. Or that *he* wanted to be the only one to tease her and make her laugh.

It was just because he was afraid she was vulnerable. That she'd fall for the next guy who came along. That she was desperate to find a father for her baby. Which was fine. The baby obviously needed a father. But Perry wasn't the right one. Neither was Joe. He couldn't think of anybody who'd be good enough for her or for the baby.

''No,'' she said, ''but the new rule might bother your new housekeeper.''

''Ms. Bloomberg?''

''She just asked me for a list of the single men on the ranch.''

"What the hell for?" he asked, his eyebrows drawn together. "You know I deliberately chose an older woman for the job."

"Why? Do you think older women aren't attractive? Don't want a man in their lives? Aren't interested in...in..."

"In sex?" He ran his hand through his hair until it stood on end. "I don't know. I told you I don't know anything about women."

"That doesn't stop you from having opinions or from giving orders," she noted. She put one hand on her slightly rounded belly and drew in a quick, sharp breath.

"What is it? What's wrong?" he asked. "What are you doing, standing there like that? Sit down." He took her firmly by the shoulders and eased her onto a bale of hay next to the barn. Then he lifted her legs and stretched them out on the hay in front of her, his hands lingering on the undersides of her knees.

"See what I mean?" she said, tilting her head back against the weathered boards. "Orders. Always orders."

"You didn't answer my question. Is anything wrong?" he asked with a frown. He crouched down next to her and placed his palm against her forehead. "You feel warm."

She reached out and touched his cheek. "So do you," she said with a catch in her voice. "That makes two of us." Her hand was soft and smooth. A smile curved the edge of her lips, so sweet and so inviting it made his heart pound. He leaned down. She leaned forward. The sun beat down on the back of his neck. The sweet smell of hay mingled with the scent of flowers. Her scent. The look in her eyes invited him, tempted him. He cupped the back of her head with his broad hand and slowly, slowly brushed her lips with his.

The hunger spread through him like a wildfire. He

wanted to kiss her, really kiss her, until he'd set her on fire, too. Until she wanted him as much as he wanted her. Warm? Warm didn't begin to do it. It was heat he felt. Heat from a bonfire.

She felt it too. She must have. Her lips met his at last in a wild frenzy of passion. Her hands linked around his neck, pulling him close, closer until she filled his senses. Until he couldn't think of anything but Mallory. Couldn't want anyone but her. His tongue stroked her lips until they parted and let him in to the sweet, dark recesses of her being.

She moaned deep in her throat. The sound urged him on. She was flat on her back now, and he was on top of her. He kissed her eyelids, her forehead and the corners of her mouth. She tasted like sunshine and flowers, and he couldn't get enough of her. She raked her fingers through his hair. His reaction was swift and strong. His jeans were uncomfortably tight against his throbbing arousal. He thought of taking her up to the loft where the sun shone through the crack in the roof. Where it was quiet and they could make mad passionate love with the dust motes dancing in the air. There was straw everywhere, in her hair and sticking to her shirt.

But before he could do anything to realize his fantasy, the ground shook and the earth tilted on its axis. It took minutes before he realized it was the galloping horses in the far distance that made the ground shake and not the pounding of his heart. He looked over his shoulder. It was the crew riding back for lunch, still on the horizon. He swore under his breath. With a huge effort, he sat up and pulled her with him.

Her eyes were glazed, her cheeks flushed. She pulled a stalk of straw from her hair and studied it with shaking fingers, studiously avoiding his gaze.

"There's more where that came from," he said.

"That's what I'm afraid of," she murmured.

"Don't be afraid," he said, skimming his hand across her sweater, grazing the swell of her breasts. If the horses hadn't been galloping toward the barn and their lunch, if his crew wasn't getting closer and closer, he might not have had the willpower to get to his feet. But they were and he did.

He held out his hand and she took it. She stood and faced him. But she kept her gaze averted from his. She fastened her eyes on his collar. He put his hands on her shoulders, turned her around and brushed off the seat of her pants, his hands lingering on the sweet curve of her hip.

The men arrived at the barn, hot and dusty and hungry and curious, just as Mallory walked away slowly and deliberately with every shred of dignity she could muster. She brushed casually and ineffectively at her jeans as she went down the path. The laughter and loud remarks rang in her ears. She was glad she'd escaped. Zach could take the kidding and the raunchy comments. He was the boss, for heaven's sake. For all her newfound confidence, her ability to give orders, she was still just a housekeeper's assistant.

She could face them later. After she'd picked the straw out of her hair. After her hands had stopped shaking. After her face had stopped flaming and her heart had stopped pounding. She could face them. But could she face Zach? The men didn't know what had happened. They could guess, and they probably would. But Zach knew. He knew she'd lost her head. He might even have known that in one more minute she'd have been tearing his shirt off so she could feel his warm skin against her palms. Yes, she'd have been begging him to make love to her. He knew now how weak she was, how easily she could fall for the first man who came along.

She thought she'd learned her lesson. She'd assumed that from now on she'd recognize a dangerous situation, that she'd learned to beware of rugged, good-looking men. But she didn't know her body would betray her. She told herself it was the pregnancy that made her exquisitely sensitive to his touch. That made her acutely aware of the way he looked at her. That made her want him as she'd never wanted any man.

It had to be hormones and chemistry. What else could it be? Otherwise she would have walked away, as her brain had instructed her, before she ever sat down on that bale of hay. It was the twinge she'd felt, right under her ribs, that caused her to sit down in the first place. Now it was gone and she had no more excuses. No more reason to wrap her arms around him and kiss him and fantasize about making love to him. From now on it was going to be strictly business.

She knew one thing. Zach was not Joe. Zach was something else. Despite his loveless background, or maybe because of it, he cared about her. He didn't want to, but he did. Why else would he keep her around, forbid her to lift, and worry about her health? Because he felt responsible for her. Nothing more, nothing less.

She checked out Joe's old cabin. She looked at the rooms without really seeing them. Someone had cleaned it. And made the bed. This time she felt no regret as she looked at the bed and the cozy little living room. Only relief that he'd gone and spared her a loveless marriage. She stepped outside to pick wildflowers and stuck them in a jar on the small dining table. Then she headed back to the house to wash the straw out of her hair before lunch.

* * *

Zach piled a hearty helping of chicken and dumplings on his plate, only vaguely aware of the various conversations circulating around him. He told himself that if Mallory didn't want to come to lunch it was none of his business. He had other things to worry about. Lost cows. Broken fences. A sick bull. Then there was his new housekeeper who wanted a golf cart and his octogenarian foreman who hadn't even shown up yet.

But he couldn't keep his eyes off the door. Couldn't stop wondering where Mallory was. Couldn't keep from heaving a sigh of relief when she finally did slip in and take her place at the end of the table next to Perry, that lecherous old coot who was instantly all over her like glue. She'd changed her clothes, he noticed. She was wearing shorts with a hip-length linen shirt.

There was no trace of hay in her hair that he could see. Her face was scrubbed clean, devoid of makeup. He didn't know how she managed to look young and innocent and sexy at the same time, but she did. His heart hammered, remembering how lush and ripe her body was and how her kisses made his blood race. And how close he'd come to violating every rule he'd ever made for himself. Someone on his left asked him about a new saddle. On his right they wanted to know about the rodeo. His mind was blank. All he could think about was Mallory. How her lips tasted, how she felt pressed against his body and how much he wanted her. So much his whole body ached.

He couldn't stop staring at her, wishing she'd look up. He was afraid he'd offended her, that he'd used his power as her boss to take advantage of her. He had to talk to her. Explain that it wouldn't happen again. It couldn't happen again. As much as he wanted it. It just wouldn't work. There would be talk. There might be talk already, if the knowing looks on the faces of the wranglers when they arrived at the barn were any indication. He couldn't afford that. And she didn't deserve to be the object of any speculation.

Juana passed a basket of hot rolls around the table and refilled the iced tea glasses, and still Mallory never looked his way. Not even when he rapped his glass with the end of his knife. "For those of you who haven't heard about the personnel changes, please welcome our new housekeeper, Cass Bloomberg," he said. "Cass will be taking the place of Mallory."

"Where's Mallory going?" somebody asked from the end of the table.

"No place," he said firmly, trying to catch her eye. "Mallory will now be the assistant housekeeper, in charge of the main house and kitchen."

Cass raised her hand. "I'll be doing the rest of the housing, so if there are any problems..."

Instantly the air was filled with suggestions for improving the TV reception, complaints about clogged gutters and the quality of the drinking water. Requests for new carpeting, furniture and roofing followed. Zach tapped his glass again.

"Let the poor woman eat her lunch," he said. "You can talk to her later about your individual concerns."

Cass nodded. And lunch proceeded. Zach noticed Mallory was eating. And that Perry was bending her ear. He only hoped the guy wouldn't distract her from getting the nourishment she needed.

Perry look up at Zach. "What's this about a no-fraternization rule, boss?" he asked loudly. Silverware clattered. There was a buzz around the table.

"Fraterna...what?"

"What's that mean?"

"Don't apply to me."

Then the room got quiet. Everyone turned to look at Zach. Including Mallory. Her cheeks were flushed.

He glared at Perry who gave him a smile that bordered on a smirk. Why hadn't *Perry* run away with Diane? He was good at what he did, but he was also a pain in the butt.

"Now that we've got these two beautiful ladies here, I hope you didn't mean what you said about no fraternizing," Perry said with a mischievous twinkle in his eye.

"The new rules are still being worked out," Zach said. "I'll keep you posted."

"But what does it mean?" Cass said with a worried frown.

"I'll explain it all later," Zach said. When he'd had time to formulate something that would keep the men from bothering his two new female employees and still keep everyone happy. Reasonably happy. He didn't want to send anyone packing. He couldn't afford to lose any more valued help, but he couldn't have any more of them running off together, either.

If the look on his new housekeeper's face was any indication, any no-fraternization rule wouldn't go over well with her. And he needed her desperately. So maybe there would have to be special exceptions to the rule. How did he get himself into these things? Just when he should be concentrating on his cattle, he was embroiled in personnel problems. They'd gone for years with no rules, and now, because of these two new women on the ranch, everything was different.

Conversation around the table went back to normal. Everything was normal—except the way he felt when he looked at Mallory. Guilty for taking advantage of her. Angry with her for letting another man take advantage of her. And tempted, so tempted to kiss those lips again, to get her alone, to find out if she wanted him as much as he wanted her.

But first he had to apologize for what happened at the barn. He'd explain that he'd lost his head. That it wouldn't happen again. Not unless she wanted it to. He knew what he'd say, he just had to find a time to say it. Without anyone else around. After a dessert of mountains of fresh strawberry shortcake, he saw her push her chair back from the table, and he casually got to his feet. If he timed it right, he could run into her in the hall and continue with her on down to her room.

But just as she disappeared through the door, Slim Perkins walked in. The old guy appeared to be extremely spry for his age. He tipped his hat and introduced himself to everyone who was left at the table. And Zach was stuck for another half hour answering Slim's questions while his frustration mounted.

He would have gone to see Mallory, but he had to spend the afternoon showing Slim around. The guy was not only spry, he was sharp. He'd had years of experience and it showed. He picked up on Zach's problems with his cattle, diagnosed the malaise that had seized the bull and seemed grateful for the small cabin which was now his.

"Flowers," Slim said, noting the bouquet in the jar on the table. "A nice touch. A woman's touch, unless I miss my guess," he said.

"That would be Mallory," Zach said.

"She the portly woman with the gray hair?" he asked.

"No, she's her assistant."

"Young? Pretty?"

"Well, yes, but..."

"I'll have to thank her in person," Slim said with a gleam in his eye.

Zach clenched his back teeth together to keep from mentioning the no-fraternization rule. He excused himself and left Slim to settle in.

Mallory spent the afternoon in the kitchen. Tex gave her a list of supplies he needed and told her where to get them. She sat on a stool at the chopping block making lists, while Tex rolled dough for blueberry pies.

"Boss's favorite," he said.

"You'll have to teach me how to make that crust," she said, admiring the way he fluted the edges.

"Way to a man's heart..." Tex said with a grin that showed his gold tooth.

"I'm interested in pie, not men's hearts," she said, absently drawing hearts around the items on her list.

"What's going on here?" Zach asked, barging in through the back door.

Mallory dropped her pencil. She was hoping she could get through the afternoon without running into him. Without having to explain her actions in the barn. She was having a hard enough time explaining them to herself.

"Just a little fraternization," she said lightly.

Zach scowled.

"It was a joke," she said, picking up her pencil. "This is strictly work. I'm making a shopping list just like Diane used to do." She wanted to smooth the frown lines from his forehead. Wanted to make him smile again. Wanted him to look at her like she was a desirable woman. Instead of the way he'd glared at her at lunch, like she was a poor replacement for the esteemed Diane.

"Can I talk to you?" he asked.

"Sure." She propped her elbows on the scarred chopping block and looked up at him.

"I mean in private."

She shrugged and slid down off the stool. She wiped

her damp palms against her shorts and walked out the back
door into the kitchen garden with its climbing runner
beans, its leafy spinach, and clusters of squash. She didn't
want to talk to him in private. Or even in public. She could
only imagine what he'd say. He'd lecture her on fraternizing with the staff. He'd tell her to eat more. To worry less.
He'd tell her he was sorry he'd kissed her that morning.
She braced herself because she could see it coming.

He pointed to a wooden bench in the middle of a patch
of budding green peas. She sat down.

"If it's about what happened this morning," she began.
"I'm sorry."

"*You're* sorry?" he asked.

"You'll have to excuse my behavior. You won't believe
this, knowing what you know about me, but I usually
don't...do what I did."

He stared at her in surprise, but she didn't look at him.
Instead she dug a hole in the soft dirt with the toe of her
sandal.

"You mean kiss me?" he asked.

She nodded.

"Why did you?" he asked.

"I've been asking myself that all morning. I think it's
my condition. I can't seem to control my emotions, my
hormones are all messed up."

"So it has nothing to do with me? You would have
kissed anybody that came along?"

She paused. "I don't know about that. You're a very
attractive man and you're good at kissing and I guess, of
course it had something to do with you. It had everything
to do with you." Her voice was so soft he barely heard
her. Her honesty unnerved him and set his heart hammer-
ing. He sat down next to her on the bench, cupped her
chin and forced her to look at him.

"Anyway, I enjoyed it," she confessed.

"You *enjoyed* it?" The woman knew how to provoke him and drive him over the edge. How dare she *enjoy* a kiss that had left him only frustrated and half-satisfied and hot and hungry for more. "What about this?" he demanded. He kissed her again, his mouth devouring hers. This time it was a searing, soul-searching kiss that dared her to chalk it off to hormones.

She pulled back and gazed at him, her eyes glazed and her face flushed. She was breathing hard, trying to catch her breath. She could say what she wanted about hormones, or about "enjoyment," but there was the flame of desire burning in her eyes. He recognized it because it matched his own. And he could only blame it on lust— pure and simple white-hot lust. He wanted her so badly it hurt. It hurt even more to know he couldn't have her.

"What happened this morning was my fault," he said. "And *I* can't blame it on hormones."

"Then what?" she asked, edging back to the far corner of the bench. "You feel sorry for me?" The look in her dark eyes dared him to offer her sympathy.

"I thought of that." He rubbed his hand across his forehead as if he was still thinking about it. "But I feel sorry for a lot of people and I manage to keep my hands off them," he admitted ruefully.

"It doesn't matter," she said. "What matters is that it won't happen again. Not outside the barn or in the kitchen garden. Not anywhere."

"Why not?"

"You know why not. I'm your employee. And there's a rule about…"

"Forget the rule. It's unenforceable."

"All right. But there's the matter of my pregnancy. And my future. I can't afford to get involved with anybody at this point. And I'm the last person you should get involved with.'' She shook her head.

''Who should I get involved with?'' he asked, reaching out to run his thumb along the sensitive skin under her jaw. Feeling the pulse in her throat leap to life.

''I don't know,'' she said, her voice dropping to a whisper. ''You know I can't...I can't think when you do that.''

He dropped his hand. He couldn't resist a smile. So his powerful feelings weren't all one-sided. He didn't think she'd ever admit it.

''I'm just an astronomer,'' she continued in a tremulous voice, ''not an astrologer. And I know less about men than you know about women. But if you ask me who you should get involved with...''

''I did ask you,'' he said.

''Then you shouldn't get involved at all. You said nothing was as important to you as the ranch. Nothing and nobody.''

''It's true,'' he admitted grudgingly. But suddenly the ranch seemed so big, so hard to control, so amorphous, and Mallory was so close, so sexy, so desirable.

She got to her feet and paced back and forth between the rows of corn. ''I like it here,'' she said. ''I like my room and I like Tex and the wranglers and I think I'll like my job, too, once I get the hang of it.''

''What about me?'' he asked.

''Yes, of course I like you, too. But if I'm going to stay here for the next five months...''

''You are,'' he said.

She glanced at him. She hadn't known him very long, and she didn't know him very well, but when Zach Calhoun used that tone of voice there was no point in arguing. Not that she wanted to. She wanted, *needed* this place until her baby was born.

"As I was saying," she said, planting her feet in the soft dirt. "If I'm staying here then we have to have some kind of rules."

"Let me tell you from the voice of experience that there's no point in making a rule you can't enforce. Especially if it has to do with men and women."

"This has to do with you and me."

"All right," he said, his hands on his hips. "Let's hear it."

"One, no stargazing together."

"How am I going to find Venus without you?"

"Zach…" she warned. Already her resolve was crumbling. When he dropped his "I'm the boss" attitude he was almost irresistible. That was why they had to have these rules.

"Go on."

"Two, no physical contact."

"What if you faint again?"

"I won't. I promise. That was from the shock. I'm over the shock."

"But are you over the guy? Are you over Joe?"

She stopped pacing and looked at Zach, surprised by the anxiety in his voice, by the taut worry lines around his mouth. "Yes," she said. "There wasn't anything to get over really. I never loved him. I didn't even know him."

"Good," he said brusquely.

He was obviously relieved. But only because he didn't want her fainting all over the place, she figured. "Back to the rules. Number Three. No personal discussions between us. Only business."

"Such as?" he asked, folding his arms across his waist.

"Matters pertaining to the ranch. The kitchen, the workers, the laundry, the groceries."

"Won't that get a little boring?" he asked.

"I'd rather be bored than..."

"Than what, Mallory?" Blatantly ignoring Rule Number Two he ran his hands slowly down her arms causing every nerve end to react to his touch. "Than aroused, excited?"

She shivered. Yes, she was aroused. Yes, she was excited. If he got any closer, her resistance would be down to zero. She'd have no way to stop him from breaking every rule she'd ever invented. And making sure she broke them, too.

"Yes," she said firmly. "I'd rather be bored."

He dropped his hands. "Okay, Mallory, you win," he said. "If you're sure that's what you want."

"I'm sure," she said. Then turned and walked back to the house. If she stayed one more minute, she'd have to confess she wasn't sure about anything, least of all what she wanted from him.

She wasn't sure she could get along without any physical contact, not sure she'd be happy with no discussions of a personal nature, and definitely unsure about stargazing without him. He'd been an enthusiastic learner, seemingly interested in everything she had to say about the stars. But maybe it was all an act.

She walked through the kitchen without noticing Tex was kneading bread, through the dining room without noticing Maria setting the table for dinner, right past Juana vacuuming in the living room and back to her room to contemplate life on the ranch without attention from her stubborn, headstrong, sexy boss.

For the next week he wasn't around. And he was right. She *was* bored. She heard from Maria he was out negotiating a water rights deal with his neighbor to the south. She couldn't help feeling hurt he hadn't told her himself.

She found herself listening for his car in the driveway, but when he came back, he was in nonstop meetings with his lawyer in his office.

Then he left for L.A. in a private plane that landed in the pasture to pick him up for the cattlemen's meetings. And he never had time to look her up, or to ask how she was doing. He'd taken her rules to heart. Not only that, he wasn't even around to follow them. Well, that's what she wanted, wasn't it?

She ordered groceries and took an inventory of the household supplies in the big house. But without him around to run into in the stable or to stare at her from the head of the dinner table, or surprise her with an unexpected appearance in the kitchen, life seemed unexpectedly flat and yes...boring.

It did give her the opportunity to snoop in his bedroom on the second floor, however. Of course she didn't call it snooping. She called it taking inventory. With Juana she counted sheets and towels in the linen closet. And when Juana went down to the laundry, Mallory opened the door to Zach's room and stepped inside.

The walls were paneled in rich walnut. The view from the huge window was Calhoun ranchland, rich and lush and undulating all the way to the horizon. Fresh air rustled the plain white curtains. So this was where he looked out over the land he loved more than anything. More than anyone.

She inhaled deeply the scent from the black leather ottoman at the foot of the bed mingled with the smell of wool from the hand-knotted Turkish carpet. There was something else in the air. The all-male scent of Zachary Calhoun. It lured her, it enveloped her. Mallory's knees buckled, and she grasped the post at the foot of his bed for support.

The bed was huge, what else would one expect from a man who was six feet three inches tall? And covered with a thick navy blue comforter. So this was where he slept. She pictured his long, lean body under the smooth muslin sheets. Bare shoulders, bare chest... What else? She tiptoed to the walk-in closet and opened the door, her stomach churning with trepidation.

"Just taking inventory," she murmured to herself, closing the door behind her.

Work clothes were stacked on shelves. Shoes were in boxes. Suits and jackets and slacks on hangers. Underwear on shelves. Boxer shorts. The walls were lined with pungent cedar that tickled her nose.

Downstairs a door slammed. Footsteps on the stairs. The bedroom door opened. Her heart pounded. He was home. And she was in his closet. She was going to sneeze. She clapped her hand over her mouth and held her breath. But it was no use. Her muffled sneeze sounded like a gunshot in her ears. He jerked the closet door open. She froze like a deer caught in the headlights.

Six

"**W**hat the hell?" he demanded.

"Just taking inventory," she murmured, her face flaming.

"Of my clothes?" His dark eyebrows drew together.

"Yes…no." She stepped out of the closet, trying to pretend it was an everyday occurrence to be caught in your boss's closet. "I mean I'm dusting. I don't lift and I don't throw. But I do dust. I'm the assistant housekeeper in case you've forgotten."

He scowled. "I haven't forgotten," he muttered. "I tried, but I couldn't."

He gave her a long look, from the top of her head, down her hip-length shirt to her elastic-waist shorts to her painted toenails. Then back up again, his gaze lingering on her breasts that were getting heavier and fuller by the moment. Did he notice that her belly was expanding? That her body was humming with awareness now that he was here and they were face-to-face? If she had any sense she'd run from the room. If she had any sense she never would have come into the room at all.

But she was here and she wasn't leaving. Not yet. She'd missed him too much. He was back, looking bigger, taller and more rugged than she remembered.

"How's everything going here?" he asked, leaning back on the heels of his boots.

"Fine," she said lacing her fingers together. "You didn't tell me you were going away."

"What was the point? You wouldn't have kissed me goodbye, would you? No, it's against the rules. Let's see, was it Rule Number Two or Three?"

"I might have made an exception," she admitted softly, dropping her eyes to study the geometric pattern on the carpet. She was ready to make an exception right then and there. If he didn't kiss her soon, she was going to kiss him. That's how desperate she was. Call it hormones, call it lust, she didn't care, she had it bad for Zach Calhoun.

She'd been dreaming about him, dreaming of his mouth on hers, imagining a long, slow and steamy kiss. She knew dreams didn't come true, but she was getting desperate. She'd give him two minutes to close the distance between them and then she was going to take action. She'd throw her arms around him. She'd kiss him and tell him it was a welcome-back kiss to make up for the goodbye kiss he missed.

She could almost feel his arms tighten around her. She ached to feel the warmth of his body pressed against hers. It might have been her condition. It must be her condition, because she'd never felt like this before. Whatever it was, she wanted him. She reminded herself she couldn't have him. He wasn't taken, but he wasn't available.

Zach took a step forward and narrowed the gap between

them. Mallory was so close he could feel the heat from
her body and smell the haunting floral scent that followed
her everywhere. He wanted to touch her, he wanted to kiss
her.

He'd been thinking about her nonstop, through the ne-
gotiations and during the meetings. He'd never before let
anything or anyone distract him like this. But here was this
woman, pregnant with someone else's child, and he
couldn't get her out of his mind. He'd worried about her,
wondered if she was overworking, lifting when he wasn't
there to check up on her. And he worried whether any of
the other men were hitting on her.

"Any fraternizing going on in my absence?" he asked
casually, resting his hands on her shoulders.

"Well, Cass hangs out in the bunkhouse at night. She
plays bridge with Slim and some of the other boys. Is that
what you call fraternizing?"

"No," he said. "Where do you hang out?"

"In my room with my books or in the kitchen with
Tex," she said primly. "He's teaching me to bake."

He dropped his hands to his sides. "You haven't been
up on the hill with your telescope?"

"It's been cloudy. But maybe tonight..." She walked
to the window and glanced out. "Look," she said, "I'm
sorry about all those rules. I had no business...I mean
you're the boss. You make the rules."

He went to the window and stood next to her, looking
at her while she looked at the cows grazing under the trees.
"No, you were right. You have the right to set limits."

"Maybe, but I missed talking to you, not just about the
ranch, but about...about personal matters."

"So, Rule Number Three, out the window," he said,
unable to tear his eyes away from her, from her profile,
her softly rounded cheek, her straight nose and determined

chin. His gaze dropped to her breasts and her belly. He
was fascinated by the way her body had ripened and filled
out in just the short time he'd been gone. He was aching
to touch her, to cup her breasts, to span his hands across
her stomach.

"Then there's Rule Number Two," she said, still studiously avoiding his gaze while her cheeks turned pink.

"Another rule out the window?" he asked. "Let's see,
which one was that?" As if he didn't know. He caught her
chin and turned her face in his direction, forcing her to
meet his gaze. A warm wind blew in the window and
ruffled her hair. She didn't answer the question. She didn't
have to. He knew the answer. He saw it in her eyes.

That's not all he saw. He saw longing there, and needs
and wants she couldn't hide, and all the control he'd been
holding in check snapped. All the frustration of the past
week welled up and threatened to choke him. Before she
could say anything, he pulled her close and took her soft
lips in a hard kiss. He heard her gasp, and then she
wrapped her arms around him. Her fingers laced around
his neck, her body pressed tight against him.

Her heart was racing. So was his. The heat from her
body flowed through him and back to her. It was more
than physical attraction, this feeling he had for her, much
more. It went deep, so deep he didn't know what to call
it. A wave of possessiveness swamped him. He wanted to
make her his. He'd never felt this way before. About anybody.

He traced her lips with his tongue. She moaned softly
and opened her mouth to him. Her tongue met his and they
tangled together. Her hands were in his hair, she was pulling him close, closer. His pulse thudded in his ears. Did
she know what she was doing to him? Did she have any

idea that she'd tripped the switches he'd turned off years ago? Did she know where this was leading?

"Mallory," he whispered hoarsely, his lips brushing her cheek. "We stop now, or we don't stop at all." Pulling back slightly, he waited in the silence that ensued.

He'd been scared before. He'd been scared of being thrown off a wild horse. He'd even been pinned to the fence and almost gored by a bull. But he'd never been this scared. Scared she'd say yes, more scared she'd say no.

"Don't stop," she begged breathlessly, clinging to him.

He backed toward the door, taking her with him, unwilling to let her go for even the few seconds it took to close and lock the bedroom door.

He paused, leaning against the door, his arms loosely holding her around her waist so she could escape at any time. "Are you sure this is what you want?" he asked, his eyes searching hers. The eyes that looked into his were glazed with passion.

"Are you?" she asked.

He trailed hot kisses down her cheekbone to the hollow of her throat where her pulse beat frantically. "Yes," he muttered.

She pressed her forehead against his. "Me, too." Her breath was hot against his face.

They lurched across the floor together, as if they were welded together, as if they were both afraid to let go. Because if either one let go they would only be half a person. They were headed toward the bed, and he stopped at the edge, sat on the dark blue quilt and pulled her toward him. She gripped his shoulders and arched toward him. He fumbled with the buttons on her shirt. Then he peeled her shirt off and gazed at her breasts spilling from her skimpy lace bra. He groaned. He had to have her.

He reached out and cupped her creamy white breasts in

his palms. They swelled and peaked until they filled his broad hands. His breathing sped up and his throat hurt from wanting her so much. Her body, so full and so ripe, called to him in the most basic and primitive way. He buried his face between her breasts and tugged at her shorts and her bikini briefs.

Her heart thudded. His heart pounded. Her hands were in his hair. He couldn't wait much longer.

He'd never seen anything so beautiful as Mallory. Never wanted anything as much as he'd wanted her. He ran his thumbs over the rosebud tips of her breasts. She made a funny little sound in the back of her throat, and her knees buckled.

He stood up, lifted her off the floor by the elbows and set her on the bed. He yanked at his jeans, but he couldn't get them off fast enough. She sat cross-legged, watching him struggle with a glazed look in her eyes. She was totally naked and totally unashamed. He was hot and throbbing and just as unashamed.

When he'd finally shed every scrap of clothing, he was fully aroused, and he didn't know how long he could wait to possess her. He felt like he'd already been waiting half his life. But she deserved to be seduced. He refused to think she'd already been seduced. He refused to think about Joe. He hoped to God she wasn't thinking about him, either.

Mallory sat staring at him, her very breath sucked out of her body. Her face paled at the sight of his beautiful body, so obviously ready to make love to her. He stood staring at her as if she was a statue instead of a living, breathing woman who was filled with desire. Self-conscious, she crossed her arms over her breasts. As if she could hide them from him.

She looked into his blue eyes and saw white-hot flames

of desire. Flames that ignited her. That made her feel like she was on fire. She refused to worry, refused to think of the future. All that mattered was the here and now. All that counted was what happened in this bed now.

"My God, you're beautiful," he breathed. She dropped her arms. Her shyness gone.

But suddenly she had a momentary flash of panic. She'd had so little experience. And he knew it. Maybe he had enough for both of them. Though she'd rather he'd had none. Never slept with anyone. Saved himself for her. No, that was ridiculous. Ludicrous.

"What's so funny?" he asked, coming for her at last across the big bed. He cupped her face between his broad hands and trailed kisses along her forehead, down her jaw and along her throat.

"You... me," she said. "Isn't this what you meant by fraternization?"

"I'll show you what I mean by fraternization," he muttered. He braced his hands on the mattress and continued his voyage of exploration, his kisses getting hotter and hotter. His mouth found her puckered nipples and teased and suckled until she couldn't think, couldn't breathe.

She was losing control. She wanted him inside of her. She wanted the empty void to be filled with him. Now.

"Now," she said. "I want you now."

"I want you ready," he returned, his voice hoarse.

"I'm ready," she breathed.

He feathered kisses down her curved abdomen to the juncture of her thighs. She trembled. Oh, so gently he reverently parted the petals of her femininity with his callused fingers. She was warm and slick and waiting for him. She *was* ready. He caressed the nub, the core of her being. The tension was unbearable. Building and building until she broke apart, split into a thousand pieces. She called out his name. And burst into tears.

Zach lifted her to him, held her tight against his chest, his own needs forgotten. "What is it?" he asked. "What's wrong?"

She sobbed uncontrollably. The tears streaked down her cheeks. He kissed them away, he tasted their saltiness. But he tasted no regret. No sorrow.

She shook her head. She couldn't speak for a long moment. Finally she lifted her eyes and took a deep shaky breath. "I didn't know. I had no idea."

"First time?" he said, incredulous that she had never experienced the peak of pleasure before.

She nodded, avoiding his gaze, suddenly shy again.

"Hell, what kind of men—"

"Only one."

"Oh." He didn't have to ask who it was. Anger and the urge to protect her, to take away her past hurts, filled him. He knew he couldn't undo what that bastard had done to her, but he could try. Starting right now.

He soothed her with soft words, he told her how beautiful she was and how much he wanted her. Hell, he didn't have to tell her, she could *see* how much he wanted her. When her tears were dry, he traced circles around her dusky rose nipples and watched them peak and bud.

"You're incredible, you know," he muttered. "So responsive."

"I'm responsive to you. Only you," she whispered, her voice filled with wonder. "I want you so much."

Her words shot through him like a jolt of lightning. He braced his arms again so his weight wouldn't crush her, and she arched forward, waiting, wanting....

He sank into her at last, into her warm, wet, willing body. He felt her shudder beneath him, and with each thrust she gasped with pleasure. He couldn't believe how well he fit her. She was like a sleek glove around his masculinity. He watched her face, saw her lips part, her eyes gaze up at him with pleasure. His thrusts grew deeper and harder. She reached for his shoulders and dug her nails into his skin. Then came the tremors as she tightened around him, and he exploded inside of her.

He rolled over, taking her with him so she was lying on top of him. Exhausted, spent, his whole body shook from the sheer emotional high he was on. She buried her face against his neck.

There was a pounding in his ears. It got louder and louder. Mallory raised her head. She heard it, too.

"Boss...boss? You in there?" It was George, his handyman, knocking on the bedroom door. "Telephone."

"Take a message," he growled.

"It's Diane. Calling long distance."

"I'll call her back."

Mallory sat up, her face flushed, her hair a tangle, her body still tingling.

"You'd better answer it," she whispered.

"Yeah," he said, running his hand through his hair. "She might be in trouble. I'll be down in a minute," he yelled.

He got off the bed and thrust his legs into his jeans. "Stay there," he ordered, buttoning his shirt and unlocking the door. *You'd better answer it*, she said. Why not take a message? Because Diane might have news of Joe. Mallory was still interested in Joe. Of course she was. It was only natural. He was the father of her child.

Mallory's whole body trembled as a cool breeze wafted through the open window. It was just a cool breeze, but it might have been an Arctic wind from the way it affected her. She reached for her clothes on the floor and got dressed but it didn't help. The chill came from deep-down inside her. Yes, Zach had only gone to answer the phone, but she felt alone, deserted, and forgotten.

She knew one thing. She never would have left him so abruptly no matter if God himself had been on the phone. Not after what they'd been through together. Not after what she and Zach had shared here in his bedroom. Obviously it meant nothing to him because he'd left her to answer a telephone call. From Diane! Sure, Mallory had told him to answer it but that didn't mean she wanted him to. Did she really expect her to sit there naked and wait for him to return? If so, he had another think coming.

She looked around his high-ceilinged, super-masculine room, feeling small and insignificant and out of place. As she buttoned her shirt, she dragged herself to the door, knowing she didn't belong here. Not in his bedroom, not on his ranch and definitely not in his life. She never had and she never would.

Hadn't he told her in no uncertain terms there was no room for a woman in his life? Not her, not anybody. So why was she here in his bedroom? Because he was everything she admired in a man. Cool, competent, kind and caring. This was not just another one-night stand. Because she was not the same person she was five months ago.

She wasn't the same and neither was the situation. In some ways it was worse. Last time it could have been anyone. Because last time she'd been out to prove she was a desirable woman. That she could attract a man physically. That she could follow through with it. This time it was different. It couldn't have been anyone. It couldn't have been anyone but Zach.

Last time she forgot about Joe the minute it was over. Until she found out she was pregnant. This time she wouldn't be able to forget about Zach. Wouldn't ever be able to forget how he'd made love to her and how he made her feel. Desirable, beautiful and loved. Even though he didn't love her.

She sighed and slipped out the door. There was no one in the hall. No one on the stairs. She went to her room, washed up and combed her hair. The face in the mirror was flushed and soft and fuzzy around the edges. The eyes that looked back at her were suspiciously bright and wise and knowing at the same time.

"What do you know now," she asked her reflection sternly, "that you didn't know before?"

Her lips curved in a smile. "Everything," she murmured. "Everything there is to know."

It didn't take long for her to come down off her high. For her to realize she knew nothing. Nothing except this affair they'd embarked on was going nowhere. She wouldn't have to tell Zach. He knew as well as she did. She was leaving in five months, he was staying. She was starting a family, he didn't want or need one. He had the ranch.

She didn't see Zach until dinnertime. Seated at the end of the table as usual, he looked at her just as often as he looked at anyone else. Maybe less. He didn't say anything about Diane's phone call. Maybe because it was too personal to discuss at dinner. Though he must know how anxious she was to know why she'd called. The conversation centered around cattle, the ranch and the cattlemen's association dinner Zach was giving the next week.

"It will mean extra work, but I'm sure you're all up to it," Zach said. "For those of you who weren't here last year—" he glanced at Cass and Slim and Mallory "—when our association meets in town, I usually invite the members up here for a barbecue on the patio."

"How many people?" Mallory asked, wondering what she'd be expected to do.

"Seventy-five to a hundred."

She gasped.

"Don't worry. There are two of you this year. Diane handled it all by herself last year."

She wanted to say yes, but Diane was a wonder woman and she and Cass were just ordinary human beings. She wanted to ask where Diane was this year and what she'd wanted on the phone. But she just sat there, pretending a dinner for one hundred people was no problem. Pretending they'd never made love just hours ago, just as Zach was doing. But she wasn't as good at pretending as he was. Her hand shook as she buttered her corn bread. He was calm, cool and unperturbed.

She walked out of the dining room with her head held high, and Zach didn't try to stop her or speak to her. She went to her room and told herself she didn't care. This was how she wanted it. This was how he wanted it. And this was the way it had to be. What happened up there in his bedroom had been like an explosion. Nobody'd planned it, nobody could have stopped it, either.

Of course she was still shaking. That's what happened in the aftermath of an explosion. It would take a while to get over it. Maybe a day or two. She read astronomy journals, at least she held them up in front of her eyes until she couldn't keep her eyes open any longer, then she went to bed.

The next day Zach was gone again. Nobody told her he'd left. He didn't leave her a note. She didn't see him leave, either, but she knew he wasn't on the premises. She never used to have ESP, but she had it now. It could be her pregnancy, or it could be something else. She didn't question her new ability to intuit people's presence or non-presence, she just accepted it.

Just as she accepted her role as assistant housekeeper. She ordered food for the barbecue. She consulted with Cass, she talked to Tex and the maids. The days that followed were clear, but the nights were cloudy. Finally, several days later, she stuck her head out the window after dinner and looked at the sky. Not a cloud to be seen.

She picked up her telescope with one hand and her collapsible stool with the other, and though it was only twilight, she headed out of the house to the hill she'd chosen as her own outdoor observatory.

"Where do you think you're going?"

She was so startled she dropped her camp stool. Her ESP had failed her. She hadn't known he was there.

"Stargazing," she said coolly, quickly regaining her composure.

Zach came up behind her, picked up her stool and took the telescope out of her hand. "I thought I told you not to carry things."

"I didn't know you meant my telescope."

"Now you do," he said. He glanced at the sky. "Isn't it a little early for the stars?"

"It's not too early to see Venus."

"Good. I've always wanted to see Venus." He followed her up the path.

When they got to the top, he set her telescope down and Mallory pointed to the horizon. "There it is," she said, unfolded her camp chair and sat down.

He stood staring at the brilliant planet for a long moment, his feet planted wide apart. "I've been away."

"I noticed," she said. Then bit her tongue. Why couldn't she play it cool? Pretend she hadn't noticed whether he was there or not.

"Did you?" he asked. She didn't answer. Finally he spoke again. "I came back to the bedroom," he said. "But you were gone."

She adjusted the lens on her telescope with fumbling fingers. "Yes," she said. "I had work to do. I couldn't hang around as if I was your...your..." She struggled for the right word to choose. There were so many things she was not. She was not a real housekeeper, not an astrologer, not his mistress, not even his lover. Unless one becomes a lover in one afternoon. During one incident. One passionate incident. How should she know?

"As if I were your...concubine," she said at last.

"A concubine?" he said, stifling a smile. "Where did that come from? Nobody would ever call you a concubine."

"Why, because I'm pregnant?" she asked. How dare he laugh at her?

"Because nobody knows what it means," he said. "Mallory, what happened between us that day was only between us. It was an incredible, fantastic experience. At least for me."

"Was it?" she asked softly. "I thought it was, too. But I'm not an expert."

"And it's nobody's business but ours."

"So far. But if we kept it up it would be just a matter of time before somebody found out. And then everyone would find out."

"*If* we kept it up?" he asked. "Have you already decided we're not going to?"

"You know as well as I do, we can't have an affair on this ranch and keep it a secret."

"We could try," he said, his tone level.

"No, we can't. Pretty soon everyone's going to know I'm pregnant. Right about the same time they find out, somebody's going to figure out what's going on between us. Then what will they think? They'll think you're the father.''

"Let them think whatever they want.''

"You don't mean that. This is your home, the place you love more than anything. The people here are your family. You don't want them to think you got me pregnant and then let me go as soon as the baby's born.''

"I wouldn't do that,'' he said. "If the baby were mine.''

"Wouldn't you? Of course I could tell them it's not yours, it's Joe's.''

"No,'' he said shortly.

"Then we have to quit right now. The people who work here respect you. You want to keep that respect.''

"So you think I'd lose their respect if I had an affair with you?'' he asked, watching her through narrowed eyes. "Or is this your way of blowing me off?''

"It's not going to work,'' she said, ignoring his question. She didn't know what she was saying anymore. She just knew she had to break it off. Before it got out of hand, before she lost her head and fell in love with someone who would never love her, never marry her. Then where would she be at the end of four months? "I can't sneak around your house making love to you, however enjoyable it is.''

"If you say enjoyable one more time,'' he said through clenched teeth.

Her eyes widened. "I'm sorry. What was I supposed to say? Thrilling, exciting, awesome?''

"Not if you don't feel that way.''

"It doesn't matter what I feel. I've got to think of my future. I want to leave here with no strings attached. I want to walk away with no regrets. As soon as the baby's born I have to leave. I can't hide out any longer. I have to face the music, go back to work, get back to real life.''

"You don't think this is real life?"

"Not for me." She was proud of how positive she sounded. But when she looked up at the darkening sky and thought about leaving this place with its clear air and dazzling stars and her very desirable and sexy boss, she felt a pang of real regret. How did she know what was real life and what wasn't?

"Who's going to take care of the baby?" he asked, his brow furrowed.

"I haven't figured that out yet. I've still got some time." She turned back to her telescope and pulled her notebook out of her pocket. "Meanwhile, back to work."

She thought he'd leave. She hoped he'd leave. She thought he'd say, *That reminds me, I have work, too.* Instead he sat on the ground, leaned back on his elbows and looked up at the sky as if it was the most fascinating sight in the world. To her it was. But to him, she'd bet her life that a herd of purebred cattle surpassed the sight of the evening sky.

In the falling darkness, she studied the outline of his body: his long legs, his broad shoulders, as relaxed and graceful as one of the mountain lions that roamed these hills. And just as dangerous to her peace of mind. As if he had nothing better to do than lounge on the grass and look at the stars. She knew he had plenty to do.

She looked at her star chart. And thought about his hands, so rough and callused from hard work, and so skillful and so possessive on her tender flesh. She peered through her telescope, flipped a lever so she could take a series of photographs with the attached camera of one of the summer constellations she could study later. And remembered how his kisses brought her over the edge. She pressed her hand against her beating heart. She glanced to her left. He was still there. How on earth was she going to concentrate with him there?

"Don't you have something else to do?" she asked.

"Plenty. But I came up to see something. Since I have an astronomer on my staff, I ought to take advantage of it. Tell me something. What's on the agenda for tonight?"

"Tonight? You really want to know?" She was surprised at his interest and pleased beyond normal expectations. "Tonight we'll be able to see the summer constellations, Sagittarius, Scorpius, maybe even Libra. But not until later. Until it gets dark. In the meantime, there's Venus."

"She's the goddess of love, right?"

"So they say. I'm an astronomer, not an astrologer, no matter what people think."

"If you were, I'd ask you what was in store for me," he said.

"It doesn't take an astrologer to tell you what's in store for you. You're going to acquire more cattle and more land and become even richer and more successful than you are now."

"What about my personal life?" he asked, turning his head to look at her.

She sighed loudly. The last thing she wanted to talk about was Zach's personal life. She raised the lens on her telescope and leaned forward, but she saw nothing. Nothing but frustration. Nothing had ever interfered with her work before. Nothing and nobody.

"That gets more difficult. If I tell you, will you leave?"

"If you promise not to carry your telescope again."

"All right. All right."

She saw him smile in the dark, his teeth gleaming white as a wolf's. She gave a little shiver of apprehension. Whatever she told him he'd dismiss as garbage. Which was exactly what it was. But it was worth it if she could get rid of him.

"Here goes," she said, tilting her head back to look at the sky. "Mars and Venus and Neptune are fighting it out in your relationship house. I don't know who will win. It's your choice. Problems? Other people would kill for your problems. You already have everything you want."

"That's not true," he said, his voice deadly serious. He got up off the ground, slowly, casually. He ambled up behind her and put his hands on her shoulders. Strong and possessive hands that gripped her and held her like he'd never let her go. A shudder went through her body. Desire leaped like a flame, so sudden it shocked her by its intensity.

She turned slowly on her stool. He pressed her face into his muscular thighs. Into his aching throbbing masculinity. She stifled a moan from deep in her throat and threw her arms around his legs.

Zach groaned. And broke her hold on him. It took every bit of willpower he possessed. If he hadn't, he would have taken her on the ground, right then and there, and made love to her again. Under the stars, on the grass, with Venus rising and giving her blessing. He wanted, needed to taste her mouth again. To feel her silky hair brush his fingers, to skim her breasts with his fingers, to cup their fullness, to hold the weight in his hands.

What a woman. A bundle of ripe, ready womanhood combined with a wide-eyed naïveté that was almost his undoing. Her delightfully uninhibited response to their lovemaking had left him shaken and wanting more. He'd thought about her constantly while he was gone. When he'd come back to the bedroom that afternoon and found her gone, he wasn't surprised. She was as skittish as a new foal. But he had been disappointed. And he had to face it, he had felt blue ever since. Yes, he had everything he wanted. Everything but her.

He'd only moved a few inches away from her, but it was a start.

"Look, Mallory. I can't get involved with you," he said. "You know it. I know it. Everyone knows it. You're leaving when your baby is born. It's what you have to do." What he didn't say was he'd already had two women leave him. She knew that. He didn't tell her that he'd recovered nicely. She knew that, too. She also knew he wasn't about to go through it again, thank you very much. He wanted her, yes. More than he'd ever wanted anything. But he didn't need her. He didn't need anything or anyone.

"I'm going down to the house," he said, his voice tight and controlled. If he could only control his traitorous body as well. "I'll be back to get your telescope in an hour. Don't even think of carrying it yourself. Is that understood?"

She stared at him. Her lips parted, as if she was going to speak, but she didn't. She just shrugged. He turned and walked away.

When he came back an hour later, she was cool and calm. And so was he. As cool and calm as he could be when his heart was pounding like a jackhammer. Side by side, they walked down the hill without talking. She resented his carrying her telescope. He knew that. What more she resented, he could only imagine.

She cleared her throat. "I didn't get a chance to ask you. What did Diane want?"

"To give me her forwarding address."

"Which was?"

"A post office box in Oregon."

"Did she say anything…"

"About Joe? I didn't ask. I didn't know you cared." He couldn't keep the acid note out of his voice. He'd made love to her only a few days ago, blotting out every other woman he'd ever made love to, and she wanted to know about Joe.

"I don't care. I just wondered. After all, I live in Diane's room, I sleep in her bed, I'm doing her job…sort of. Is it so strange that I'm curious about her? That I want to know if she's still with Joe? If she has a job?"

"I guess it's not strange you should ask about her. She asked about you."

"Me?" she asked, startled.

"She asked if I'd found a replacement for her. I told her I had."

"I hope you told her it took two to fill her shoes," Mallory said.

"I told her you were doing a great job," he said.

"At what?" she asked, slanting a glance at him in the dark.

"At *everything*," he assured her.

"If you said it like that," Mallory said, "she'll wonder."

"Wonder what?" he asked.

"If anything's going on between us."

"But there isn't," he said. "Not according to you."

"Don't tell me you don't feel the same," she said. "You said it yourself. You can't get involved with me. I understand perfectly. It's not a good idea to have an affair with your assistant housekeeper who's pregnant with your ex-foreman's baby."

His gave her a rueful smile. "When you put it that way…"

"What other way is there to put it?"

She glanced up at him and stumbled on a root.

He dropped her stool from his left hand and grabbed her arm. Then he set her telescope on the ground. God, she was so beautiful with the moonlight shining on her hair, gilding her features. "You could put it this way," he suggested. He drew her close and slanted a kiss across her lips. Her lips were cool. She didn't respond. She was holding herself aloof. Keeping her emotions in check. After what he'd said, he didn't blame her.

He admired her self-control. At the same time he wanted to shatter it. He wanted to see her come apart at the seams. He nibbled at her lips, coaxing, seducing until she breathed a long shaky sigh and gave in. Almost. Within moments, she caught herself, braced her hands against his shoulders and said, "No."

"You're right," he said brusquely. "It's wrong." What was wrong with *him*, that he kept coming back for more? When he knew there was no future in it? It was her. She was driving him crazy.

He picked up the telescope and carried it to her room. He didn't say anything. She didn't say anything. There wasn't anything else to say. Then he went to the kitchen, poured a glass of milk and took it to her room. It was not an excuse to see her again. It was just to make sure she got enough calcium. When she opened the door, she was holding her side and her eyes were glazed with tears.

His blood pressure skyrocketed. "What's wrong?"

"It's the baby. He...he kicked me."

He almost dropped the milk. "Oh, my God. Does it hurt?"

She sat down on the edge of the bed and smiled through her tears. "No, it just startled me. I thought at first it was something else. But it isn't like anything else."

He put the milk on the dresser and sat next to her. She gasped and grabbed his hand.

"There he goes again," she said, lifting her shirt and placing his hand across her bare stomach.

He felt the kicking of a tiny foot, and his gut twisted. "There's a baby in there," he said, staring at her and moving his hand lightly over her stomach.

She laughed softly, a lilting sound that made him crazy with desire. That made the blood start racing through his veins again.

"Yes," she said, and wiped a tear from her eye.

There *was* a baby in there. Joe's baby. He couldn't let himself forget it. Before tonight the baby had been an abstract complication. Now it was real. A real baby with wants and needs of its own. Anger welled up in his chest— at Joe for leaving. At his father for leaving his mother. And there was something else. A raw pain that ripped through him and almost felt like jealousy. It couldn't be. He'd never wanted a baby. He still didn't. There was no room in his life for a wife, let alone a child.

If he was jealous, it was because he hadn't been Mallory's first lover. Her eyes were gleaming, brimming over with some unnamed emotion. She was so lovely, so vulnerable. How could anyone take advantage of her vulnerability? Had he done so himself?

"Are you okay?" he asked.

She placed her small hand over his large one that was still splayed over her stomach. "I'm fine. I'm glad you were here."

The warmth of her hand on his, her firm round belly under his hand caused the heat to rush to his groin. Lust, combined with possessiveness, threatened to swamp him. He knew the pride of possession. He was proud of the land he owned that he'd inherited and developed on his own. But he'd never wanted to possess a person until Mallory came along. Now his feelings seemed to extend to her baby, too. This worried him. Hell, it scared him to death.

"I wanted to tell somebody, but I didn't know who," she said.

"Now you know." He rubbed his thumb over her stomach. She drew a quick breath and closed her eyes. Her breasts rose and fell with her deep breathing. His hands itched to feel the weight of them. He lifted her legs and stretched her out on the bed. He wanted to stretch out next to her, to take her in his arms, to make love to her again. To lose himself in her welcoming warmth. This time it would be slow and lazy. He reminded himself that she'd said no. Only recently. Less than an hour ago.

"When's your next doctor's appointment?" he asked.

Her eyes flew open. She looked at him as if she'd forgotten he was there. She yanked her shirt down to cover her bare stomach. "Why? I'm fine."

"I know you're fine. I just want to know what the doctor says."

"Do you still insist on coming with me?"

"That's right."

She sighed and sat up. "It's the twenty-second."

"I'll be here." Reluctantly he got off the bed and handed her the glass of milk.

She handed it back to him. "I can't drink milk all by itself."

"You're being difficult."

"At least I'm not overbearing and bossy."

"I have a right to be bossy. I'll remind you I'm the boss."

"I have a right to be difficult. I'll remind you I'm pregnant."

"You don't have to remind me," he said, his eyes skimming her body, lingering as he noted the subtle changes. The glow of her skin, the widening of her hips.

"I'm getting bigger, aren't I?" she said, her face flushing under his scrutiny. "I feel like a cow. A pregnant cow."

"What's wrong with that?" he asked, continuing to let his gaze take a lazy tour of her body. "Pregnant cows are beautiful, too."

"You think I'm beautiful?" she asked after a brief pause.

This was not a ploy to get a compliment. He could tell by the wistful tone in her voice, she really wanted to know. He could have told her she was the most beautiful woman he'd ever seen. That her face haunted his dreams, that her body with its rounded curves drove him wild with desire. But he didn't. He couldn't. Flattery, compliments, sweet talk. They weren't his style.

"Not as beautiful as a pregnant cow, but I'll say this, you come close," he assured her with a grin.

She threw her pillow at him. He ducked, and it landed on the floor.

"Not only difficult," he said, "but childish. You're regressing into childhood. Are you going to blame that on your pregnancy, too?"

"At least I have an excuse. What's your excuse for being an overbearing bully? And don't say it's because you're the boss. Other bosses are kind and supportive. They're team players."

He choked on a laugh. "Where did you hear that?"

"I didn't hear it, I know it," she said, tossing her short curls. "This may be the first time I've been in the housekeeping field, but I've had jobs before, lots of jobs, working my way through school. And I've had lots of bosses."

"And none of them were as overbearing as I am?"

"No. Well, there was one who came close, but I have to say, you're the most...the most..." Mallory searched her mind for an appropriate adjective she hadn't used before on him.

"But none of them was as good-looking as I am, either, were they?" he asked with a teasing grin.

"All of them," she assured him. "Some were better looking. Male models, movie-star quality. Of course in a certain light you look like a movie star, too."

"I do?" he asked, his grin broadening. "Who?"

"Did you see *The Bride of Frankenstein?*"

His grin faded. His eyes narrowed. "You'll pay for this, Mallory Phillips. I *was* going to the kitchen to get you a piece of chocolate cake to eat with your milk, but now..."

Her mouth watering, she jumped off the bed and brushed past him on her way out the door. He'd gone too far. Just the mention of Tex's three-layer chocolate cake made her stomach grumble. She left him standing in the doorway, watching her hurry down the hall.

When she came back, after two pieces and a large glass of milk, she found a note on her bed saying he'd be gone for a few weeks to Montana and to tell George to carry her telescope if she wanted to go up the hill at night. He signed it "THE BOSS. AND DON'T YOU FORGET IT."

"Orders, more orders," she muttered, licking the cake crumbs off her lips. But deep down she was touched by his solicitude. No one had ever cared about her welfare like this. She reminded herself that it was only his sense of responsibility that made him do it. It had nothing to do with her. And everything to do with the fact that Joe was the father of her child and his foreman. He would have taken care of the Bride of Frankenstein if she'd been alone and pregnant. Wouldn't he?

Seven

The next time Mallory saw Zach was the day of the barbecue. She and Tex and Cass worked together on the prep-
arations. They hung lanterns from the trees around the
patio. Actually George hung the lanterns while they
shouted instructions.

"A little higher."

"More to the right."

"Over there."

The wonderful smell of slow-roasting beef was wafting
from the six-foot-long, covered barbecue stand. Baked
beans were simmering in electrically heated pots. There
were platters of marinated vegetables and bowls of potato
salad. Everything looked and smelled delicious to Mallory.
She was always hungry these days. Tex had noticed. He
beamed at her when she came into the kitchen late at night
for a snack. He made special treats for her, things he knew
she liked, like sticky buns and chocolate pudding.

"Not afraid of getting fat?" he asked one late night in the kitchen while Zach was gone.

She looked down at her stomach. "I'm afraid it's a little late to worry about that," she said.

"Any reason for that?" Tex asked kindly.

"I'm pregnant," she said. There, it was out. And it wasn't so hard to say the words after all. "I haven't told anyone else. Except Zach, I mean."

Tex raised his eyebrows.

"It's not Zach's baby," she said quickly. She was right. She knew that was the first thing that would come to mind.

"Oh, I see," Tex said. But she could tell he wasn't convinced.

There was no way she could convince him Zach wasn't the father, unless she told him who was the father and she wasn't going to do that. Not ever. So she let it go. Knowing everyone would speculate, but no one would know for sure. Unless she told them.

After telling Tex, she told Perry and Cass, and pretty soon everyone knew about her condition. After her initial embarrassment, she had to get used to everyone acting like she had some rare and wasting disease. They'd pull her chair out for her at dinner, they'd pass the salad bowl to her first, but they wouldn't let her hold it. They almost wouldn't let her butter her own bread.

She decided it couldn't last. They'd grow tired of babying her, almost as soon as she got tired of being babied. They'd also get tired of guessing who the father was. At least she hoped they would.

Mallory stood outside, arranging the flowers for centerpieces on the round tables set up around the patio. Her fingers fumbled with the carnation stems. Flower arranging wasn't her forte, but since she wasn't allowed to carry out so much as a napkin from the kitchen, she got the job. As she jabbed the last flower into the last vase, she heard the sound of cars in the driveway. At last the cattlemen were arriving from town. And with them, her boss.

With damp palms, she smoothed her sundress with the spaghetti straps and Empire waist and decided she'd be better off in the kitchen. But she never got there. Cass assigned her to the salad table. She wanted to hide. What would she say to a bunch of cattlemen? What would she say to Zach?

Welcome back?

Hi, I missed you?

Everyone knows, and they think it's yours?

Everyone knows, and I wish it was yours?

Did you miss me?

It turned out she didn't say anything to him. Not at first. He was playing the genial host. Several people looked at her with curiosity. She smiled and heaped potato salad on their plates. Zach didn't speak, but he looked at her. She caught his gaze across the patio. And held it for a long moment. The air was charged with positive ions. Her skin prickled. She tried, but she couldn't take her eyes off him.

He did look like a movie star in his Western shirt. And it wasn't Frankenstein as she'd jokingly told him. It was George Clooney combined with Matthew McConaughey.

"Boss is having a good time," Tex said as he carved her a slice of beef off the grill. "He likes to entertain. Show off his spread."

Speaking of spread...she looked down at her waist, what there was left of it. The next thing she knew Zach was at her side, his arm clamped tightly around her. She gasped and would have dropped her plate if he hadn't taken it from her. He pressed her so tightly against his side she could feel his ribs and the muscles in his arms under his blue chambray shirt.

He smelled of hay and horses and fresh air even though he'd supposedly been in meetings all day. He was too close. Too possessive. He made her whole body throb. She'd been thinking about him nonstop since he left, but she wasn't ready for him yet. She needed some time to get used to his being back. To bring her raging emotions under control. But here he was, so big, so strong, brimming with confidence and pride and breathing fire.

"Come and eat with us. I want you to meet some people."

"I don't think so."

"I do. You said yourself you needed to get back to the real world."

"That was a long time ago," she protested.

"Change your mind?"

"No, but I didn't mean now, I meant later, after..."

"If you wait till after it may be too late. You'll have forgotten what it's like in the real world. Besides, Stella has been telling everyone you can read the stars."

"Not her. Is she here?" She peeked over his shoulder.

"She's the vice president of the association. Come on, you don't have to tell anyone what house their stars are in if you don't feel like it."

She paused. He hadn't ordered her to come, not yet, but he might. "But what if they notice...?" She glanced down at her stomach.

"Notice that you're the most beautiful assistant housekeeper I've ever had?"

"I'm the only assistant housekeeper you've ever had," she reminded him tartly.

He snapped his fingers. "That's right. I forgot. Look, I don't give a damn who notices what. You look better with every passing day. Pregnancy becomes you. Don't you know that? And even if they do notice, they won't say anything. They may be hayseeds and yokels, but unlike me most of them have a few manners.''

She couldn't help the smile that tipped the corners of her mouth, and he took that to be a yes. Before she knew what was happening she was seated between Zach and a short, round-faced man with deep creases forking off from the corners of his eyes.

"Mallory, meet Harper Jones. Mallory works for me."

"Lucky you," Harper said to Zach. Then he turned to Mallory. "What do you do?"

Mallory opened her mouth to say she was the assistant housekeeper, but Zach cut her off.

"She's an astronomer."

"Really? Why do you need an astronomer, Zach?" the man asked.

"He doesn't," Mallory cut in. "I'm really here to..."

"To help me identify the stars and the constellations. To make sure the earth keeps spinning on its axis. That kind of thing."

Harper's puzzled gaze moved from Zach to Mallory and back again.

"I don't know how I ever got along without Mallory," Zach continued, resting his hand on her bare shoulder. "Before she came I never even knew about the nebulae. They're basically just dust clouds, you know," Zach said. He glanced at the sky.

"Where?" Harper asked.

"You can only see them with a telescope," Zach said. "And with a powerful telescope you can even see the intergalactic nebulae."

Harper looked dazed and got up to refill his plate.

"Why did you go on like that?" Mallory asked under her breath. "You bored him silly."

"That's not why he left. He was just hungry."

"And where did you learn about the intergalactic nebulae?"

"It's common knowledge."

It wasn't common knowledge. Zach knew that. He'd stopped at the observatory on the campus when he was in town and made some inquiries. He wanted to see the place where she'd worked. He wanted to see his competition. He wondered if he had a chance of keeping her on the ranch in some capacity. Not as a housekeeper, but what? He wouldn't marry her, he wouldn't marry anybody. Ever again. But he liked having her around. *Liked* was not the right word. He craved her presence. Like air or water, he needed her there.

"Who are all these people?" Mallory asked, looking around at the noisy crowd.

"Some are friends, some just business associates. All important to me." He almost said, *but not as important as you,* but he caught himself in time. He wouldn't say it, he wouldn't even think it. He hadn't realized how desperately he'd missed her until he saw her there. Then he couldn't stay away, couldn't keep his hands off her. These were old friends he wanted her to meet, some dating back to his uncle's time. They were here last year and they'd be back next year. They were the constants in his life. Along with the ranch.

Mallory would be gone next year. Back to her old life. Back to "reality." He told himself to get up and circulate, but he couldn't tear himself away from her. Her skin glowed as if there was a candle inside her. He ran his finger lightly over her shoulder and up the back of her neck. He loved to feel her soft curls, loved to see her reaction to his touch. Her cheeks colored, her breath quickening.

"What happened while I was gone?" he asked, his lips close to her ear.

"Let's see," she said ticking the items off on her fingers. "Cass beat Tex at bridge the other night. Tex found a new recipe for Swedish pancakes, and the barn cat had kittens."

"I mean what happened to you? Any more word from you-know-who?" He dropped his gaze to rest on her rounded stomach.

"Ohhh." Her face flushed. "He's an active little guy."

"How do you know he's a guy?"

"That's funny. I don't. I just assumed from the way he kicked..."

"Does it matter?"

"No," she said thoughtfully. "He or she can be a soccer player."

"Or an astronomer," he suggested. *Or a rancher,* he thought, but he didn't say it. If he had a child, he'd want him or her to inherit the land. However oblivious to his parental responsibilities his uncle had been, he'd been proud when Zach took over the ranch. Zach remembered what he'd said just before he died.

"It's all yours, boy," his uncle had said. "Just keep it in the family. Promise me that."

Zach had promised. At the time he hadn't yet married, but assumed he would. Assumed he'd have his own kids. Assumed his wife would raise them since he didn't have a clue how to do it. That was a lot of assumptions ago. A lot of assumptions and a lot of disappointments.

Talk of the baby made Zach want to put his hand on her belly. To lift her shirt and run his fingers over her smooth skin. The memory of her baby moving beneath his palm had resonated somewhere deep inside him and stuck with him these days he'd been away. He'd be talking about crossing shorthorns with Charolais and suddenly Mallory would cross his mind. Her skin, her scent, her body. Her baby.

He couldn't put his hand on her. Not now. Not here. Someone might notice. He wanted to spirit Mallory away and have her all to himself. Either in his room, her room or the hill under the stars. But he was the host, and he had an obligation to act like one instead of some lecherous landowner.

He took her hand and pulled her to her feet. He took her around the patio, stopping to talk and introduce her around.

When Stella saw her, she let out a little shriek. "There she is," Stella said. "Over here, Mallory. She's so amazing. She knows everything."

Zach watched Mallory stiffen. But Stella had her sitting at her table and before Zach knew what was happening, Mallory was telling their horoscopes. She caught his eye, gave a tiny shrug of her slender shoulders and continued inventing advice and foretelling the future.

He stood next to the barbecue stand, arms crossed over his chest and watched. Wishing he hadn't shared her with the world after all.

"Pretty amazing, isn't she?" Tex said as he scraped the grill. "What's gonna happen to her?"

Zach shook his head. "I don't know. Why don't you ask her?"

"I did. Said she was going back to the university."

"The real world is what she told me," Zach said.

"Hah. This world is real enough for me," Tex said, glancing at the patio with its grape arbor and lanterns. "She makes herself useful. Everybody likes her. Why can't she stay?"

"She can." *But she won't.* "Women don't stay on the

ranch, Tex. I don't know why, but they don't. Take Diane, for example. I thought she'd be here forever. I should have known. They all leave. Sooner or later. If Mallory's going to leave, it might as well be sooner.'' He kept his tone level, but Tex gave him a sharp look as if he knew about the hollow void beneath his ribs. As if he knew that just thinking about her leaving made him feel empty inside. Picturing her taking her baby and walking out of his life was even worse.

"About the baby," Tex said. "She gonna marry the father? And don't say ask her, 'cause I already did. She said no."

"Then why are you asking me? Oh, you think I *am* the father?"

"It occurred to me," Tex said. "And some other folks."

"I'm not," Zach said flatly. *But I wish I was.*

"So, if you're not the father and she's not gonna marry the father, why don't you marry her yourself?"

Zach turned to face his cook. If he'd suggested Zach join a monastery, he couldn't have been more astounded.

"Why don't I what?"

"You heard me. Marry Mallory."

"One, she isn't interested in me." *Not interested enough. Not enough to stay there.* "I'm her boss. That's all."

"Then why does she look at you the way she does? Like you're some kinda superhero...and ask about you, what you were like as a kid, and..."

"Because she's interested in people. She asks about everyone." *Including Joe.* "Two, I've been married. It didn't work out."

"So? Everybody gets two chances. Maybe more."

"Not me. I got one chance and I blew it," Zach said.

Tex raised the height of the grill and threw another piece of meat on it. "You didn't blow it, she did."

"That's not what she said. She said I ignored her, spent all my time on the ranch."

"But you've changed," Tex insisted.

"No, I haven't. I still spend all my time on the ranch. I still love this land. Nothing can compete with it. Nothing and nobody. Is that clear?" Zach didn't wait for an answer, he strode over to a group of ranchers and joined the conversation. Why did he have to explain something so obvious to someone he knew so well?

He made a supereffort to forget Mallory and concentrate on the business of cattle and the cattlemen who were his guests. When he finally turned to look for her, she was gone. His disappointment was acute. He wanted to find her, but the guests lingered. He was hot and bothered, and his frustration built. He thought of turning the lanterns off. Of cutting off the supply of coffee and after-dinner drinks. He was getting desperate.

Finally they left. He stood in the driveway, watching the cars and trucks disappear down the road, and heaved a sigh of relief. But Slim was waiting for him to tell him there was a problem with the power supply in the barn. By the time they'd fixed it it was almost midnight. He stood in front of the house, staring at her window. Her bedroom light was off. Of course it was. She needed her sleep. She wasn't hot and bothered and aroused as he was.

On his way upstairs he walked down the hall past her bedroom. He paused and listened at her door. He pictured her asleep in her bed, her tousled head on the pillow. Was it hard to sleep with a baby inside you, kicking you? Did she toss and turn? Did she ever dream of him the way he dreamed of her? There was no answer from her room. He'd never know. He ground his back teeth together and went upstairs.

Eight

The next day and the rest of the week were more meetings. He was back at the ranch to change clothes, that was
all. He didn't see her. On the twenty-second, the day of
her doctor's appointment, he canceled a trip to a ranch in
Nevada and a chance to bid on a prize, championship bull.
He'd pulled in the night before and went to breakfast in
the morning, relieved to see her at the end of the table,
eating Tex's famous sourdough French toast. Always in
the back of his mind was the possibility that she might not
be there one day. That when he came back from a trip
she'd be gone. Her room empty, her car missing from the
garage. He knew it wasn't rational. He knew she was staying until her baby was born, but still...

"Gonna stay home awhile, Zach?" Perry asked him.

"Yep. It's good to be home. I've missed this place."
His gaze sought hers. *I've missed* you. *Did you miss me?*

"Gonna be around today, boss?" Marv asked. "I want to show you something."

"Yes. No. Part of the day." He had no idea what time her doctor's appointment was. He shot her a quizzical look, but she was busy pouring syrup on her plate, missing her French toast completely. So she wasn't quite as unaware of him as she acted. That was some consolation for the way she appeared to be ignoring him.

He followed her out of the dining room into the hallway and she told him the appointment was at four.

"You don't have to come, you know," she said. "I'm perfectly capable—"

"Of taking care of yourself, I know. But I'm coming, anyway. We'll stay in town and go out to dinner."

"Out?"

"Yes, out, as in out to a restaurant. I want to talk to you. Around here I never have a chance. There's always someone nearby."

"What do you want to talk to me about?"

"Hey, Zach," George yelled from the dining room.

"See what I mean?" he said.

Mallory nodded and went to the laundry to run a load of towels. It was lucky she'd bought a couple of summer dresses with Empire waistlines where the fabric floated over her expanding stomach. She'd worn one to the barbecue and today she'd wear the other. At best she hoped to look like a heroine in a Jane Austen novel, at worst she feared she looked like a baby dolphin.

The last time she'd gone to town with Zach was the day he'd hired the real housekeeper without telling her. She wondered what he'd do today. What he wanted to talk to her about. Maybe he'd finally realized that she wasn't really earning her keep. That Cass could probably do it all.

No, he wouldn't take her out to dinner to tell her she

was fired. He'd leave a note signed "The boss and don't you forget it."

When she saw Zach waiting for her in front of the house, she was glad she'd worn her new dress. He was wearing khaki slacks, a dress shirt and a tie. Clothes she remembered seeing in his closet. The memory of his catching her there and what happened afterward caused her heart to trip double time. She had to stop thinking about him. Stop picturing him *without* his dress clothes. Without any clothes at all, with his tanned broad shoulders, his chest covered with springy dark hair...

Oh, Lord, she was getting carried away. What would the doctor say when he saw her blood pressure was sky-high and she had to explain it was all because she lusted after her boss who was just out there in the waiting room?

She was lucky it was just lust and not love. She was lucky she wasn't in love with him. She was in a vulnerable state and just might think herself in love with the first man who came along. Who just happened to be him.

"Ready?" he asked, holding the door to his sports car open while his eyes skimmed over her dress.

She buckled her seat belt and smoothed her skirt. "You can just drop me off at the doctor's office. You must have things to do in town."

She stared straight ahead, but she felt his gaze on her, intense and unwavering. "I'm coming in with you. I want to talk to him."

"Her."

"Okay, her. That's why I'm going to town, to talk to your doctor."

"That's not necessary. This is a routine exam. I get weighed, my blood pressure taken...things like that."

"Will they listen to the baby's heartbeat?"

"I don't know."

"I want to hear it," he said.

"You can't. You can't come in there, only the..."

"Husbands, is that what you were going to say? Only the fathers?"

She sighed. "Yes. You'll be in the way. They won't know why you're there. Why *are* you there?" she asked.

"It's obvious. I'm there because I'm there."

"Oh, right. Now I see."

"Don't get sarcastic with me," he cautioned, "or you'll be sorry. I'll cut you off without any dessert."

"Don't threaten me," she warned, "or I'll tell the doctor you said I looked like a pregnant cow."

"I didn't say it, you did."

"You didn't deny it," she said hotly.

"I meant it as a compliment. You know that."

She sneaked a glance at him out of the corner of her eye. Instead of feeling terrible for insulting her, he appeared to be making an effort to hide a grin.

"It's not funny," she said, drawing her eyebrows together.

"I know," he said. But his grin only broadened.

And her nerves only escalated. She didn't know what he'd say or do in the office. If he wanted to hear the heartbeat, then nothing or nobody could stop him, even if they called out the National Guard, which they probably wouldn't do. They'd probably think he was some crazed ex-lover or some overprotective current lover, which wasn't far from the truth, or worst of all, they'd think he was the baby's father.

"Mallory Phillips?" The nurse smiled and opened the door to the hall that led to the examining rooms.

Mallory put her magazine down on the table, and Zach

did the same. She went to the door, and he followed on her heels. The nurse raised her eyebrows.

"Mr. Phillips?" she said pleasantly.

"Yes," he said.

"No," Mallory said. But he was already in the hallway, watching while she got on the scale.

"Do you mind?" she snapped while the nurse moved the lever to get a reading.

"Not at all," he said, leaning over her shoulder to read her weight.

"Most husbands aren't this interested," the nurse remarked.

"I'm not most husbands," he said.

"You can say that again," Mallory said under her breath. "You're not any husband."

"Would you like to wait out here until the doctor does her examination?" the nurse asked Zach.

Mallory held her breath, afraid he'd insist on coming in while she disrobed and thrust her arms into the openings of the blue plastic disposable garment they gave her.

"I want to hear the heartbeat," he said.

"Of course," the nurse said. "We'll call you in a few minutes."

"And I want to talk to the doctor."

"Certainly."

After the brief exam during which Mallory was glad to see her heart rate and her blood pressure were normal, the nurse brought Zach into the room. Mallory, feeling vulnerable and exposed, instinctively drew the blue plastic drape up over her stomach. The doctor introduced herself to Zach. After a brief curious gaze, the doctor smiled, obviously assuming he was her husband. She hooked up an amplifier, lifted the drape and placed her icy-cold stethoscope on Mallory's abdomen.

In a moment the booming of the baby's strong and regular heartbeat echoed through the room.

Zach couldn't move. He couldn't breathe. He met Mallory's gaze from across the room and they exchanged a long, intimate look. Her eyes were suspiciously bright and he knew she was close to tears. He felt a fierce protective urge swell in his chest. He had to take care of her and the baby. He had to. She gave him a teary, lopsided smile as if she knew what he was thinking and his heart turned over. When he finally found his voice, it was thick with emotion. "Is it supposed to be that fast?" he asked the doctor.

"Oh, yes. Your baby is perfectly normal, Mr. Phillips."

Zach exchanged a brief glance with Mallory that dared her to say he wasn't Mr. Phillips and it wasn't his baby. She didn't say anything. She couldn't have spoken if her life depended on it. She was listening to the thrilling sound of her baby's heartbeat. And she had shared it with Zach.

Zach finally left the room, she got dressed and they sat down together in the doctor's office.

The doctor assured them everything was going well.

"Is she gaining enough weight?" Zach asked, surveying Mallory with a critical eye.

"He's a rancher," Mallory explained, feeling a flush creep up her neck. "His job is to fatten his cattle."

"I see," the doctor said. "Well, you can relax, she's right on schedule. Just be sure she's getting her calcium and minerals."

"I will," he assured her.

"You'll both want to enroll in one of our birthing classes, won't you?" the doctor asked. "You'll learn some valuable techniques like breathing exercises."

Zach nodded. "Sounds good."

"As her coach, you'll learn the exercises and time her

contractions." The doctor leaned forward across her desk. "Couples often ask about continuing marital relations during pregnancy," she said, shifting her gaze from Mallory to Zach.

Mallory swallowed hard. "They do?" she asked. She couldn't believe she'd heard her say that. She didn't dare look at Zach. She wanted to hold her hands over her ears. Even more she wanted to hold her hands over Zach's ears, which were suspiciously red. He'd never admit it, but he might be just as embarrassed as she was.

"By using the imagination and trying new positions, most couples can continue having sex all during pregnancy."

"Really?" Zach said. "That's good to know." He reached for Mallory's hand and twined her fingers with his. She tugged, but he didn't let go.

"As long as it isn't uncomfortable," the doctor added. "As you get larger, of course, you wouldn't want your partner on top of you," she said to Mallory. Mallory turned scarlet. Again she tried to pull her hand away, but he held it too tightly.

She wanted to scream out that he wasn't her partner, that he wasn't her coach, and he certainly wasn't her husband, and that she had no intention of ever having sex with him again. Once was enough. Too much for her peace of mind.

"Yes," the doctor continued. "Sex is beneficial for the mother who may be feeling the stress of pregnancy as well as the father. Women need to realize they're still the object of sexual desire, not just childbearers."

Zach leaned forward as if he'd never heard anything so interesting. Mallory half expected him to take out a pencil and paper and make notes.

"What about men?" he asked. "Men have needs, too."

"Oh very definitely. Both partners should discuss their needs openly and frankly. That's what I tell my patients. It's a subject very often neglected. That's why I always bring it up."

"I'm glad you did. Aren't you, Mallory?" he asked, sending her a seductive smile.

She glared at him. His smile broadened. She wanted to hit him over the head with the paperweight on the doctor's desk. She wished she'd never brought him.

The doctor stood up. "I'll see you next month."

"That wasn't so bad," Zach said at dinner in a restaurant near the university. "Did I embarrass you?"

"Oh, no. Only every time you opened your mouth." Mallory deliberately glossed over the most embarrassing part of the appointment, the conversation in the doctor's office. If he had any sense of propriety, he'd pretend it never happened. "Did you have to look at me like I was your prized heifer? I expected you to ask if I should have supplementary mash or blackstrap molasses to increase my appetite."

"How do you know about blackstrap molasses?" he asked.

"I work on a cattle ranch," she explained, opening her menu.

"Do you really?" he asked. "What are you, the nutritionist?"

"I'm the resident astronomer. I make sure the stars come out at night and the sun comes up every morning."

"I thought that was the rooster's job," he said.

"Seriously, Zach, you misled the doctor. She thinks you're my...my..."

"Husband. Go ahead and say it. Why are you so afraid of it? You will get married one of these days. And you'll have a husband. Once you realize you're still a sex object and not just a childbearer.''

"Why would I get married?'' Mallory asked, ignoring the part about being a sex object. "I can take care of myself and my baby. Marriage is not in the cards for me. Not in the stars, either. Do you want to know what my horoscope is for today and the rest of my life? Saturn has dampened my Venusian tendencies. I'm to put feelings aside and pursue more beneficial avenues. And that's just what I'm going to do.''

He looked at her over his menu so long and hard she could feel the heat from his gaze across the table. Her resolve to put her feelings aside weakened. How could she, when her feelings ruled her life? Her hands shook and so did the menu. She finally had to look away. And she knew for certain in that long moment she wouldn't marry anyone. Unless it was him. She also knew beyond a doubt that he wouldn't marry anyone. Anyone at all.

"I think I'll have the lamb chops,'' she said, hiding her face behind her menu.

"Good choice.''

The food was delicious. They talked, but ignored the sensitive subjects of marriage and babies. And the most sensitive subject of all—sex during pregnancy. Mallory wondered if it was too late to change doctors. To find some uptight elderly MD who was too gentlemanly to ever mention anything so disconcerting as finding different positions for sex during pregnancy.

As Zach entertained her with ranch stories, she slowly relaxed and laughed at the antics of the wranglers and a runaway bull. Of rodeos and cattle drives. When the dessert menu came she pored over it so long Zach ordered her one of everything.

"If you don't eat it, we'll take it home.''

"But Zach..."

"Or would you rather have some blackstrap molasses?"

"The chocolate decadence and the warm apple tart with clotted cream ought to do it," she said.

As the waiter was pouring her herb tea, Mallory looked up to see two of her colleagues from the university walking toward their table. Two she hadn't seen since that fateful night she'd met Joe. She gasped and tried to hide behind her napkin, but they saw her first.

"I thought that was you," Dina said with a wide smile. "I told Rhonda, that's Mallory. How's your summer going?"

"Fine. Wonderful." She spread her napkin carefully over her lap. "Dina, Rhonda, this is Zach Calhoun."

Zach stood and shook their hands.

Rhonda gave Zach a frankly admiring gaze before she turned back to Mallory. "When I heard you weren't teaching this summer, I tried to call you, but your number was disconnected."

"Oh, right. I closed my apartment and left town to do some research. I'm staying on a ranch up in the hills. Better visibility," she said, as if that explained everything, which it obviously didn't since both women were looking perplexed. Mallory took a deep breath and plunged on. "See, the city lights act like the sun in brightening the sky, which is why we can't see the stars during the day."

"Oh," Dina said. "Well give me your number. I'll give you a call, and next time you come to town we'll get together."

Mallory hesitated and shot Zach a helpless look. She was not getting together with anyone from her past until absolutely necessary and not until the distant future. She didn't know Zach's number, and if she did she wouldn't have given it to her colleagues. She didn't want to have anything to do with them until she came back and resumed her old life. Until she'd had time to think up a suitable story to explain her unwed motherhood.

But Zach didn't read her mind, he thought she was merely at a loss for the phone number and promptly gave it to the woman. At the same time he rested one hand lightly but possessively on her shoulder. What could she do? Nothing. What would they think? She could only imagine.

"Research?" Dina said, looking at Mallory, then at Zach and back to Mallory. "What kind of research did you say you were doing?" Mallory could just see the wheels turning in her mind. And remembered how impressed she'd been when she'd first seen Zach, with his sun-bronzed face, his rugged features and broad shoulders. And how impressed she still was. He looked like the complete outdoor man, which he was. Right now they were probably thinking, *With a stud like this around, who has time for research?*

"I'm measuring some of the spiral galaxies with my telescope. I get a much clearer picture from out of town, without the pollutants and ambient light. So now I can classify some of the nebulae nearest our galaxy. It's really very exciting," Mallory finished out of breath.

"I bet it is," Dina said in a tone that intimated something even more exciting might be going on. "What are nebulae, anyway?" she asked.

"Clouds made of gas and dust," Zach said.

Both women looked at him.

"Are you an astronomer too?" Dina asked.

"Just a rancher. But I'm learning," he said.

"But I thought Mallory wasn't teaching this summer," Rhonda said.

"She's made an exception for me," Zach said.

"Just a rancher," Dina repeated, thoughtfully. "Then the ranch where you're staying...it isn't the Santa Ynez Valley Ranch, is it?"

"That's the one."

"Oh, how nice."

"Yes, it is nice." There was a long silence during which Mallory wondered if this wasn't a good time for them to leave. But instead of leaving they kept talking.

"So while the rest of us are teaching microeconomics and statistics 101 this summer, you're out at night studying the stars, I mean the nebulae, right?"

"That's right," Mallory said. "Every clear night, anyway."

"And the nights that aren't clear?" Rhonda asked.

"There's always something to do," Mallory said.

"I'll bet there is," Rhonda said suggestively.

Mallory took a sip of ice water hoping it would cool her blazing face.

Fortunately the waiter appeared at that moment with four desserts, and the two women were so busy looking at them they didn't notice Mallory was blushing. She just hoped no one was looking at her stomach, either.

"You know we were just talking about you. Remember that night we celebrated your birthday?" Dina asked.

Mallory felt the blood drain from her face. They could have gone all evening without mentioning that fateful night.

"Uh, yes, sure."

"What a night, huh?" Rhonda asked.

Mallory managed a tight smile. She didn't think they really knew what had happened when Mallory disappeared with the randy cowboy that night, but they must have wondered.

"We'll have to do it again," Dina said. "When you come back. When *are* you coming back?"

"Winter quarter."

Her friends imparted some faculty gossip, and Mallory crumpled her napkin in her lap, afraid they'd never leave.

"Well, anyway, you look great," Dina said enthusiastically. "Research must agree with you." As she said it, her gaze traveled to Zach.

"Thanks. Good to see you."

When they finally left, Zach sat down and Mallory heaved a sigh of relief and looked down at her desserts. Her appetite had fled.

"Did you have to give them your number and say 'she's made an exception for me'?" she demanded. "They're the world's biggest gossips. They're probably on the phone right now, and it's all over campus that I'm living on your ranch, probably *with* you..."

"I think they were more interested in your desserts."

"That too. Who orders four desserts unless they're eating for two? Oh, Lord...I thought they'd never leave," she said. "I was afraid..."

"They'd eat your chocolate cake?"

"They'd notice I'd gained twenty pounds."

"It looks good on you," he said with that frank, possessive look he had, that look that made her insides turn to mush. She was only glad he hadn't turned that look on her when the women were there. The possessive hand on her shoulder had been more than enough to set the gossip mill spinning.

She toyed with her cake. "What did you want to tell me?" she asked in an attempt to get her mind off her colleagues and the impression they might have gotten that she and Zach were involved and were living together.

"I picked up a catalog from a furniture store." He took it out of his pocket and handed it to her across the table. "I thought you should order a crib and whatever else you need."

"A crib? Where would the crib go?" Would she leave the hospital and go straight to an apartment in town? Would she come back to the ranch? For how long?

"Wherever you want it to go," he said with a shrug. So he didn't care if she stayed or went. If she put the crib in a rented apartment or in the corner of her room. She corrected herself. *Diane's* room.

"What happened that night?" he asked.

"What night?" she asked innocently, laying her fork down.

"Your birthday."

"Oh that night."

"Yes, that night. Was that the night you met Joe?"

"Yes."

"What happened?"

"It's not important," she said.

"I think it is."

"All right." She heaved a sigh of defeat. "It's embarrassing. But if you really want to know."

"I don't but I do," he said.

She waited while the waiter refilled her teacup and topped off Zach's coffee.

"In the first place, I never had a real boyfriend. I never even went out that much. I was always a nerd, according to my sister, Mimi. I really have had only one boyfriend in my life. And that was years ago. And he married…someone else. I wouldn't have gone out that night if it hadn't been my birthday. I'd just found out I'd been turned down for tenure because I hadn't done enough research. I'd been concentrating on teaching. Which is what

I love. I'd been concentrating on learning ever since I can remember. Which is also what I love.''

She took a deep breath. "Are you sure you want to hear all this?"

He nodded slowly, his eyes fastened on hers.

"So there it was, my birthday. I was feeling awful. I didn't get tenure, I was twenty-eight, and I was a virgin.'' Surprise flickered in his eyes. Then something else. His eyes narrowed. She took a sip of tea. She hadn't planned on telling him that last part, but now that she'd started this story, she couldn't seem to stop. She rushed on like a babbling brook that had been dammed up too long, ignoring the disbelief she saw in his eyes.

"Not that any of that excuses what I did," she assured him. "But my colleagues, those two you just met, and some others took me out to the bar, you know the one on the edge of town with the live music, to celebrate. They ordered drinks and I drank them. I usually don't drink so it wasn't long before I was feeling really giddy. There was this cowboy at the end of the bar who kept looking at me and sending more drinks over."

"Joe," he said flatly.

"Yes.''

"I think I've heard enough," he said, his blue eyes dark and hard as flint.

"I don't blame you."

"Just one more thing. How many times—"

"Just that once," she said, fighting the red-hot shame that rushed to her face, even now, months later. "Just that night in the hotel."

Zach's face darkened. His jaw tightened.

"I only saw him once after that."

"But he said he'd marry you."

"Yes, on the phone. I tracked him down when I found

out I was pregnant. Not that I expected him to marry me. Or even wanted him to. I just thought I should tell him. I didn't know...I mean I'd never been in that situation before. I was ashamed, humiliated. I felt like an idiot. But I thought he had the right to know.''

Mallory couldn't take her eyes off Zach's face. She tried to assess his judgment of her. Did he agree with her that she should have told Joe? Did he agree that she was an idiot, a naïve one at that? But Zach's expression was inscrutable.

"What did he say?" Zach asked grimly.

"He said he'd think it over and let me know what I should do.''

"What did that mean? Did you consider abortion?" Zach asked.

"No, never. Even though I never thought I'd get married, never planned to have kids, once I was pregnant I knew I'd keep the baby. It might be my only chance to have one, and I couldn't turn it down.'' She sighed.

"Anyway, I thought I'd never hear from him again. But he called me a week or so later and said he thought we should get married.''

"I don't believe it," Zach said.

"I didn't, either. I was shocked. I never expected that. I told him I didn't think so. After all, I didn't know him. He didn't know me. But he came to town. We met at a coffee shop. He said he wanted to give the baby a father and a home. And I...I confess, I thought it wasn't a bad idea.''

"He can be very persuasive, especially with women," Zach said dryly.

"He was. He talked me into it. He told me about the ranch and how beautiful it was and how I could watch the stars from up there...,''

"Or the nebulae," Zach said, drawing a smile from her.

"Or the nebulae. Right."

"So this was all his idea."

"Yes. I admit I was worried about what to do. About how I'd manage, what I'd tell people. I hadn't told anybody yet. I didn't want to tell anybody. I didn't look forward to explaining to the faculty and the students. Joe said I wouldn't have to work and after what I'd just been through at the university, the thought of hibernating for a while with my telescope at a remote ranch appealed to me. I guess it sounds impulsive and irrational, but I said yes."

"And you never saw him again."

"No, but I talked to him on the phone a few times. He told me we'd get married on his next day off. He described his cabin, and I told him when I would arrive at the ranch. I guess you know what happened next."

"You fainted in my living room," he said.

"That wasn't like me," she said. "None of it was like me. Not the me I used to know. But I'm afraid that me is gone forever. I'm not the same. I'm a different person. I'm skeptical. I'm cynical. I don't know what else, but the one thing, the only thing I know for sure, is that I'm going to be a mother." She buried her head in her hands, suddenly overwhelmed by emotion and the responsibility of this tiny baby whose heart she'd heard beating only a few hours ago.

"Don't cry. For God's sake, don't cry," he muttered. "You're better off without him."

She looked up and blinked back her tears. "I'm not crying for Joe. I didn't even know him. Marrying him never would have worked. It was a terrible idea. I know that now."

"Then you don't want me to get him back for you?"

Her eyes widened. "You would do that?"

"I could try. I could offer to double his salary. Throw in a few perks."

"But what about Diane?" she asked.

"I don't think there's anything serious going on there, from what she said to me on the phone. If you want my opinion I think Joe panicked at the idea of marriage and talked Diane into running off with him. He's very persuasive, as you know. But so am I. If you want him back..."

"I don't," she said. "But I appreciate the offer." She was shocked at the offer. She couldn't believe he'd do that. It meant he didn't want her himself. Not that she thought he did.

There was a long silence before he spoke again.

"It's not just for you that I'd get Joe back," he said.

"It's not?" she asked softly.

"It's for the baby. Before today the baby was just a...I don't know...an idea, a problem, an entity, but now that I heard his heart beat..." His voice caught in his throat and he struggled to get his emotions under control. "Maybe it's because I was raised by my uncle or maybe I'm just old-fashioned," he said, "but I think every child ought to have two parents. A mother and a father. So why don't you think it over?"

"I don't need to think it over. But you're right, Zach. I couldn't agree with you more about the two parents," Mallory said, putting her hand on Zach's arm. Just her touch sent a spiral of heat through his body. "But I don't think forcing someone to marry me will solve my problem. And it is a problem, not having a husband. But I plan to have lots of men in my baby's life. Oh, not what you think. I mean like my brother-in-law, my uncle and male friends. Maybe even you."

Maybe even you. Zach fought off a wave of jealousy at

the thought of sharing Mallory and her baby with other men.

"So no Joe?" he asked, secretly relieved. How did he think he'd be able to stand seeing her marry Joe? Or anybody?

"No," she said in the soft darkness.

They rode through the dark night with four desserts in boxes in the back seat. Mallory took off her shoes, tilted her head back and closed her eyes. Zach glanced at her profile and his heart hammered in his chest. Asleep she was even more beautiful and almost irresistible. If he weren't driving sixty miles an hour he'd reach for her and kiss her.

He knew how she'd respond. How she'd return his kisses, how her tongue would twine with his, shyly at first, then bolder until she'd reach under his shirt and put her hands on his bare skin. He groaned deep in his throat. She stirred and smiled sleepily as if she knew what he was thinking.

He kept his hands tightly on the wheel. It was safer that way. He wouldn't go off the road and he wouldn't go off his rocker. What was he thinking? Making love to Mallory was impossible. It was insane. She had other plans for her life. He had other plans for his life. When he got her home, he'd carry her into her bedroom and put her to bed, then he'd leave. Period.

He couldn't make love to her again. It wasn't part of the plan. Not his plan or hers. His plan was to avoid getting entangled. To spend his life doing what he was good at. Raising the best cattle in the state. Expanding his boundaries. Buying more ranchland. Procuring hybrid cattle from breeders all over the world. Improving his stock.

And last but not least, avoiding women who would walk out on him just as sure as the sun came up in the morning.

His mother taught him that. She said she'd come back, but she hadn't. He'd never forget waiting for her on the front steps, night after night, week after week until he finally realized she wasn't coming back. Then there was his wife. She said she'd stay "until death do us part." But she was gone in six months. He'd finally learned that women don't enjoy being isolated on a ranch. And that he preferred the ranch to any woman. If he had to choose, the ranch would win anytime. That's what his wife had said before she left.

"You're never around," she'd said. "What am I supposed to do while you're out on the range? You prefer the cattle to me, don't you? This ranch has a hold on you no woman can compete with. I'm sick of being alone. I'm sick of being bored. I'm leaving."

Twice in his life he'd stood in the driveway in front of the ranch house and watched someone he loved, or thought he loved, drive away. And never come back. First his mother, then his wife. He'd never forget the night his mother left. And the tears he tried so hard to hide because big boys don't cry. When his wife left, it was the shock that hit him, but there were no tears. The pain was gone now, but he'd never subject himself even to the possibility of someone walking out on him again.

Mallory was a different story. And yet more of the same. One day she, too, would turn her back on him and the ranch and drive away, never to return. The difference was, she made no secret of that. She made no promises. Oh, she needed him now, at this stage of her life. And he wanted to be there for her. But this time, when she was ready to leave, he'd be prepared and ready to let her go.

He didn't love her. He cared about her and he cared about what happened to her baby. But he didn't love her or need her or depend on her for his happiness. Fortunately for him, since she wasn't in the business of helping him repeat his past mistakes. So he'd let her call the shots. Decide what she wanted from him. If she wanted him to make love to her, well, he'd oblige. Why not? That was what the doctor ordered.

She woke when he stopped the car in the circular driveway.

"I'm not very good company, am I?" she asked with a yawn as she groped for her shoes.

"I've had better," he said drily, opening her door for her.

"I suppose even one of your prize heifers is better company than I am."

"At least they listen to me when I talk."

"Have you been talking?" she asked, looking up at him.

"I've been thinking," he said.

"What about?" she asked in a low voice. As if she didn't know. She licked her lips. Her eyes gleamed in the dark. If he didn't know better he would have thought she was flirting with him.

"About what your doctor said."

"So have I," she said, a small, shy smile playing on her lips.

He paused only a moment. "Forget the shoes," he ordered, sliding one arm under her and the other around her waist. He pulled her out of the car, lifted her up and held her against him.

"I'm too heavy for you," she murmured, her arms around his neck, her face against his chest. "Do you know how much I weigh?"

"As a matter of fact, I do. You don't have any secrets from me. I know you inside and out."

Even in the dark, with her face buried in his chest, he knew she was blushing. He could feel the heat right through his shirt, setting his body on fire. The scent of her hair and her skin invaded his senses and made it almost impossible to breathe. He carried her into the house, through the living room, down the hall, into her bedroom and collapsed on her bed with her in his arms.

Nine

Nine

If he thought she'd go right back to sleep as soon as she hit her bed, he was mistaken. Her brief nap had rejuvenated her. She pulled herself to a sitting position in the middle of the bed. Her eyes sparkled. There was determination in the set of her chin. She had something in mind. He hoped it was what he thought it was. He lay flat on his back with his arms crossed under his head, looking up at her. Holding his breath. Waiting.

"You heard what the doctor ordered," she said, leaning forward to unbutton the top button on his shirt.

"You mean keeping up relations, so you know you're still the object of sexual desire?" he asked, his voice rusty as her fingers continue to work the buttons.

"Men have needs too, she told us," Mallory said.

"Tell me about it," he muttered under his breath. "What are you going to do about it?" he asked. Could this be happening to him? It had happened so many times in his dreams, he was afraid he'd wake up alone, hot and frustrated and throbbing once again. He was more afraid her concerns would come rushing back at the last minute. Concerns about what people would think, about his reputation with his employees on the ranch.

"What am I going to do about it?" A little smile tipped the corners of her mouth. "Just what the doctor said. Use my imagination. Like this," she said, peeling back his shirt. "And this." She braced her arms on either side of his shoulders, leaned forward and brushed her lips across his mouth. He kept his hands clenched at his sides. This was her idea and her scene, and he wasn't going to interfere for the world. Unless...he had to. She nibbled at his lips, tasting and testing before she moved down to trace a scar on his chest with her tongue.

"What's that from?"

"Gored by a bull," he said in a strangled voice. God, if she went any further...

But she did. She went further, down to his flat belly, shyly exploring with her mouth while she ran her hands down his arms. The bulge in his jeans fascinated her. She ran one finger around his masculinity, then struggled with the zipper, finally freeing his aching manhood. He yanked his jeans off and then his briefs. He hoped he hadn't interfered with her plans, but he couldn't be a passive partner much longer. Not at the rate his pulse was escalating.

Mallory's eyes widened at the sight of his throbbing arousal. She gasped, and in a moment had gotten rid of all the impediments between them by tossing her dress and her bra and panties over the edge of the bed onto the floor. She felt free and reckless and wild. Her aching breasts, free of constraints at last, tempted him, begged him to take them into his mouth.

"You're so beautiful," he said, his voice deep and dark as night. "You look like a fertility goddess."

She smiled a secret, inscrutable smile. A goddess's smile.

He stroked her breasts so reverently, the touch of his hands set off waves of exquisite pleasure. Then, when she was sure she couldn't take another stroke, when her nipples were so taut and peaked she thought they couldn't be any more sensitive, he took them into his mouth. And she was lost.

"Oh, Zach," she breathed.

"Oh, Mallory." His voice was hoarse and guttural.

It was like some form of divine torture. He sucked, he laved and he worshipped her swollen, sensitive breasts. His hand reached down and sought the secret place at the juncture of her thighs, moving, stroking, searching until he found the hub of her erogenous zone. She shuddered. Waves of intense feeling washed through her, so strong she was afraid she'd break into a million tiny pieces. She wanted him so badly. She was so ready. If he didn't move inside her now she'd—

Gently he settled her on top of him. Her belly, firm and gently rounded pressed against his flat stomach. He didn't complain.

"I love the way you look," he murmured. "I love the way you feel, your body on top of me." He lifted her by the shoulders and entered her, finding her sleek and smooth and waiting for him. She moved up and down in an age-old rhythm. He joined the dance, and they rocked as one. Faster and faster, harder and harder until the bubble burst and sent shock waves pulsing through them both.

As they went over the edge together, Mallory pressed her face against Zach's neck and muffled her cries. Somewhere in the deep recesses of her mind was the possibility that someone in the house might hear them. She rolled off his body, drew her knees up to her chest and shivered.

He drew the quilt up over them both, then shifted her to her side, tucking her against him, his arms around her waist. Her bare bottom was nestled against his thighs. "Okay?" he whispered.

Okay? No, she wasn't okay. This was wrong. It felt right, but it was wrong.

"What if someone heard?" she whispered.

"No one heard," he said. His breath ruffled her hair. His thumb made circles over her womb. "Except the baby."

"Oh, Lord."

"What's wrong?"

"Everything." She wriggled around to face him. His eyes were wary and watchful. Hearing her, seeing her face, he knew the doubts were flooding in, making a wedge between them where there'd been none.

"I know what you're thinking," she said. "I know I started this. It's my fault. I'm weak."

"You're not weak. You're strong," he said, smoothing her hair.

She pressed her fingers against his lips to silence him. "All my life I've been the good girl. The girl who studied and got good grades. No time for fun. No time for boys. No time for men. Mimi got the guys. Mimi had fun. I guess I always wondered what it would be like.... I guess that's partly why I fell for Joe.

"But now it's reversed," she continued. "Mimi's a wife and a mother. Mimi stays at home at night doing dishes and I'm out having a gay old time. It's funny, isn't it?" She swallowed hard. "But now I'm going to be a mother too. I didn't plan it, but it's the best thing that's ever happened to me. I've changed. Not just physically, but emotionally. I feel things I've never felt before and I cry at nothing." She buried her face in the hollow of his neck. "What's happening to me?"

He put his arms around her and held her for a long moment. She wanted to stay there forever. Safe and secure.

Finally he spoke. "You're turning into a woman with a physical side along with the intellectual. But it scares you. You don't know where it will lead. Am I right?"

"Yes," she murmured.

"Your affair with Joe is in the past. Your future stretches ahead of you. A bright future. Because you have changed. You're no longer just an intellectual, you're an attractive woman. A sensual woman. A woman who lets her feelings show."

"Yes, maybe," she said, startled by his insight. Sometimes she thought he knew her better than anybody. "But where does it end?" she asked under her breath.

He didn't say anything, but he knew the answer. It ended with her walking out the front door the way she walked in. Only this time she wouldn't be alone. She'd be taking the baby with her. The thought brought a pain like a knife in his chest. He told himself he didn't care. It wasn't his baby. He'd felt the baby kick and he'd heard the baby's heartbeat. But that didn't make it his. And Mallory wasn't his wife. He'd made love to her, he'd brought her to her first climax and he'd caught her when she fainted. But that didn't make her his either.

She let out a ragged sigh. He ran his hands down her back, soothing and stroking until her body relaxed and her breathing leveled. Her hair brushed his cheek, her breath fanned his temple. She was finally asleep. With a Herculean effort he eased her down onto the quilt and covered her with a blanket. Then he forced himself out of her bed, and stood and watched her sleep for a long moment. He wanted to get back into that bed so badly it hurt like a throbbing toothache.

But he couldn't do it. Not tonight, not ever. He couldn't make love to her again either, not until she figured out who she was and what she wanted. He thought he could, but he couldn't. Each time it was harder for him to let her go. Each time he wanted her more.

Someone had strewn his clothes all over the floor which was the reason he took so long to get dressed. But he finally shoved his legs into his pants and his arms into the sleeves of his shirt. Then he left. He went to the car, got the desserts, put them in the giant refrigerator and went to bed.

Lying alone in his huge bed, he tossed and turned, imagining he was still there with her, sleeping with her all night long. He thought about being there in the morning when she woke up. Seeing her eyelashes feathered against her pale cheeks. Kissing her eyelids and nibbling on her earlobes.

But she was right. Sooner or later someone was going to notice. Gossip would spread like wildfire. He told himself he didn't care what people said. He'd told her the same thing. But he did care. For her sake. He didn't want anyone talking about her, wondering, speculating.... So this was it. It was over. Even if she decided she wanted to continue this affair, he couldn't do it. As it was, it was going to hurt like hell when she left.

Cutting off their relationship right now would make it easier for both of them. This way when she pulled out of the driveway for the last time, it would be just the boss saying goodbye to the housekeeper—make that assistant housekeeper. Not a routine event, but not an earth-shaking

one, either. For either one of them. That was his plan and
he was going to stick to it. He rolled over but he still
couldn't sleep. He saw her face in the darkness, he felt her
fingers against his lips. But he didn't change his mind. He
couldn't.

The next morning Mallory sat staring at her image in
the vanity mirror in Diane's dressing room. She was
shocked at her appearance. Her full body, her flushed face.
Was this the "glow of pregnancy" everyone talked about?
Or was this the glow of the morning after making love?
She sighed deeply and avoided the three-way mirror for
the next few weeks. She also avoided Zach. She couldn't
have another conversation with him about why they
couldn't, wouldn't and shouldn't make love again.

Obviously he felt the same. He avoided her the way she
avoided him. She was grateful, because she didn't know
what to say to him that she hadn't said before. Didn't know
how to explain her illogical behavior that was at odds with
her logical words. She had only the same old excuses:

She was not herself.

She was ruled by her hormones.

She was desperate to feel attractive.

She was under doctor's orders.

She was also grateful her colleagues didn't call her that
week or the next, and finally she stopped worrying about
how to put them off.

Instead of carrying her telescope up the hill, Zach had
a carpenter put up a shed with shelves and a stand for the
telescope. That way she could leave it there all the time.
She was grateful for his thoughtfulness, but she missed
him, missed his company, missed sharing her knowledge
of the stars, missed their conversation and missed their
lovemaking that made her feel so desirable. Of course she

saw him at meals, but they only exchanged the most mundane comments. Sometimes when she felt his gaze on her from the end of the table, she'd look up, but when she did, he was looking elsewhere.

Zach went out of town and was gone during her next doctor's appointment. Which spared her any embarrassing questions about her "husband." She felt guilty letting her doctor think she had a husband, but since Zach was going to be her coach it didn't really matter who they thought he was.

Life on the ranch settled into a routine. She didn't worry about anything. She felt like she was in a cocoon. Everything—food and shelter and friends were all provided for her. Cass taught her to knit. Tex taught her to bake. She did a little work around the big house during the day and at night she watched the stars.

It felt strange not to be going back to school in the fall. It was the first time in her whole life that she hadn't gone to school in September, either to learn or to teach. But more and more she was involved with life on the ranch, which had a rhythm all its own. Summer faded into fall, and the cattle were moving to winter pastures. She heard the men talking about a cattle drive, about selling "feeders," which were weaned calves.

The wildflowers were gone. Tex was blanching and freezing the last vegetables from the garden. She was helping him pick the tomatoes to make sauce. With the Indian corn from the garden, she made a centerpiece for the table.

Zach wasn't there to see her centerpiece. He was away on business. He was often away. But when he was around, the tempo of life at the ranch picked up. Even though he barely spoke to her, hardly noticed her, she noticed him. Her heartbeat sped up, and she felt more alive in every pore of her being. Even the baby seemed to notice, kicking and moving about as if he, too, could feel the electricity in the air. When the baby kept her up at night, she switched on Diane's TV and watched old movies from her bed.

Then in October, Mallory signed up for her childbirth classes. She assumed Zach had forgotten about them until he showed up unexpectedly one day when she was by herself in the kitchen, stirring a vat of spaghetti sauce.

"What are you doing?" he asked.

No greeting. No explanation for his long absences. No inquiry as to *how* she was doing. Well, what did she expect? She gripped her spoon tightly so she wouldn't drop it in the sauce. "What does it look like? I'm cooking."

"Where's Tex?"

"He's gone to town to do some shopping. Can I give him a message for you?"

"Yeah, tell him *he's* supposed to do the cooking. You're pregnant. You're supposed to take it easy."

She slapped her spoon on the counter. "Oh for heaven's sake, Zach. Pregnant women have been cooking since they lived in caves and the man brought home the wild boar. Women have work to do, pregnant or not. We're designed to work in the fields up to the last minute and then have the baby right there, if need be."

"Without the childbirth classes? Without a coach to time your contractions? Without breathing exercises?" he demanded, propping his elbows on the chopping block while his hair fell across his forehead and his cool blue gaze heated up.

"Yes, yes, yes. Without anyone or anything. Not that I'm going to—"

"Damn right, you're not." He stood up straight. "When's our first class?"

"Next Monday."

"I'll be there."

Just when she was going to assure him he didn't have to be there, Marv strolled through the kitchen, said hello to Zach and helped himself to a cookie from Tex's cookie jar.

"What's for dinner?" he asked.

"Wild boar," Zach said.

Marv nodded and walked out the back door. Mallory shook her head and the phone rang.

She turned the stove off and picked up the phone. It was her sister. Mallory's number had been disconnected. Her sister had to call the university to get her new number. What happened? Where was she? They were taking the kids to Disneyland and wanted to stop and see her.

"Oh, Mimi, I'm afraid this isn't a good time to get together," she said, glaring at Zach, wishing he'd have the courtesy to leave the kitchen and let her have some privacy.

But he didn't. Instead he poured himself a cup of coffee from the pot on the stove, took a cookie from the jar and sat down at the table. He didn't look at Mallory. Didn't appear to notice that she was speaking to her sister for the first time since she'd gotten pregnant. Didn't seem to notice that she was nervous and ill at ease and wanted to be alone.

No, he casually stirred his coffee and ate his cookie and looked at a cartoon Tex had pinned to the wall as if it was the most interesting thing he'd ever seen, though judging by the frayed edges and the yellowed paper, she was sure it had been there for the past five years.

"See," Mallory said, "it would be awkward. I don't have my own place. I'm taking the semester off to do research and I'm staying at a ranch outside town.... What? Yes, of course there are horses."

Zach took his boots off and propped his feet on the

table, casually sipping coffee, but avidly listening to Mallory try to get out of seeing her sister. The sister who thought she was a nerd.

"Yes, and cowboys too," Mallory admitted, stealing a glance at Zach over her shoulder.

He gave her an encouraging smile. She turned her back on him as if he weren't there. He knew she wished he weren't there. But he *was* there and he wasn't leaving. He hadn't seen her in weeks, and he couldn't take his eyes off her. Off her body—more beautiful with her breasts fuller than ever, jutting out above her rounded belly—or off her face, much softer and more tender. Yes, maternity agreed with her. Of course he'd never seen her when she wasn't pregnant, never known her before.

He had a feeling she needed to see this sister and the sister needed to see Mallory and learn about her pregnancy. Where he got this feeling, he didn't know. He had no siblings, no parents really. No family except for his uncle, and theirs was not the usual family. So how did he know? It was something about the look in Mallory's eyes and the tone of her voice. She wanted her sister to come, but she was looking for every excuse to put her off.

Zach cleared his throat. She turned. "Why don't you invite her to stay here?" he asked.

She covered the mouthpiece with her hand. "You don't understand," she whispered. "She has a husband and two kids."

He shrugged. "There are three extra bedrooms upstairs."

"I know, but...the kids are noisy, they're kind of wild, they'll want to ride horses."

"Fine. Let them."

"You don't understand," she said, a note of desperation in her voice.

"No, I don't," he said. "But maybe I will after they get here."

"They're coming this weekend." She chewed on her lip.

"Okay," he said.

"Will you be here?" she asked.

He had the distinct feeling she didn't want him to be there. "I wouldn't miss it," he said.

She exhaled loudly and uncovered the mouthpiece. She seemed to know she'd been defeated.

"I was just talking to the rancher, the guy who owns the ranch, you know, Mimi. And he says it's okay for you and Kent to bring the kids and stay here.... Yes...it'll be good to see you, too."

Zach listened to her give directions and hang up the phone. Mallory sat down at the table across from him, her eyebrows drawn together, her lips pursed.

"I don't want her to come here. She doesn't know I'm pregnant," she said.

"She will soon." He gave her a long, lazy appraising look.

"Don't say it," she advised him tersely. "Don't mention how big I am, don't ask if I'm carrying twins, and don't ask how much weight I've gained. And *don't...don't* tell me I'm cranky."

Zach couldn't help it. He laughed out loud. Mallory was not amused.

Ten

Mallory swatted him in the chest.

"Hey, I didn't tell you you were cranky, I didn't ask you how much you weigh or if you're carrying twins."

"You laughed at me."

He reached across the table and ran his index finger around the curve of her cheek. She was all rounded curves and lush valleys. "Not at you," he said gently. "With you."

"But I wasn't laughing."

"I'm sorry, but you're cute when you're mad. Even cuter when you're cranky. I know—you're not cranky, but if you were…"

She glared at him.

"If I can't mention how big you are, can I tell you how great you look? How beautiful your skin is and how you glow and how much I'd like to—"

"No, you can't," she said, pressing her index fingers against her temples. "What am I going to tell Mimi?"

"The truth?"

"I guess so." She buried her head in her hands.

He covered her hands with his and gently took them away from her face so he could look into her eyes. He wanted to take her in his arms and hold her and tell her not to worry. He wanted to tell her he'd stayed away on purpose because he couldn't stand to look at her and know he couldn't make love to her.

"I'm afraid she won't understand," Mallory said.

"Why, hasn't she ever made a mistake?"

"Yes, but I haven't. Not until now. Her role was to be the wild one. Mine was to be the sensible one."

"Oh, yes. She's the one who does dishes at night while you're out cavorting at bars." He still felt bitter thinking of her cavorting with Joe, even though he knew she had no love for Joe and never had. He was also convinced Joe had no love for her or any interest in her baby. It shouldn't please him to think of the baby growing up without a father, but it was possible Joe would be worse than no father at all. At least that's what he wanted to think.

"One time. One night." She held up one finger. "And I'm paying for it now."

He picked up his coffee cup and regarded her above the rim. "Are you sorry about the baby?" he asked, his brow furrowed.

She rested her hand on her abdomen. "No. How can I be? I'm just sorry he won't have a father."

"Maybe he will. Maybe you will get married one day," he suggested. The thought cut through him like a knife. She couldn't marry anyone. If he was the marrying kind he'd marry her himself, before he'd let anyone else put their hands on her. But he wasn't the kind of man to settle down....

"Huh-uh." She shook her head. "I thought I told you I won't, not unless..."

"What?" he demanded, clamping his fingers around her wrist where her pulse beat rapidly like a hummingbird's wings.

"Unless I, you know, fall in love." Her voice dropped, she looked away, anywhere but at him.

"How will you know?" he asked.

"That's a good question. I think we've had this discussion before in this very room," she said, looking at the copper pots hanging from the ceiling and the open shelves with Tex's spice collection. "We need Tex to tell us what love is."

"As I recall," Zach said drily, "he wasn't much help the last time."

"I don't know," Mallory said, staring dreamily off into space as if he hadn't spoken. "I imagine that love is feeling that you want to be with the person all the time, that you miss them terribly when they're gone. That you can share your craziest hopes and your darkest fears with them and they'll understand. They'll even make you do things you know you should do but you don't want to..."

"Like inviting your sister to spend the weekend or getting enough rest when you're pregnant."

"Yes, like that," she said. Her eyes focused on his. "Wait a minute."

"Never mind," he said flatly, getting to his feet. "I know you're not in love with me."

"That would be a big mistake," she said lightly. "Falling in love with someone who loved his ranch more than anything or anyone."

"You've got that right," he said, leaning against the counter.

"Even worse, falling in love with someone who didn't know what love was," she added, glancing up briefly to meet his gaze.

"That's both of us," he said.

She stood up and faced him.. "Well, if you ever find out…let me know."

"Right," he said.

She walked around him to go back to the stove. He caught a whiff of her scent, of wildflowers and sweet summer grasses. And he couldn't let her by. He grabbed her arm. And pulled her into an embrace. He tilted her chin and expertly covered her mouth with his. He might not know what love was, but he knew what he wanted, and he thought he knew what she wanted too. He'd caught her off guard. At first she was stiff and unyielding, but in seconds she sighed and melted against him like a bar of Tex's baking chocolate.

"You've changed," he murmured, his hands gently exploring the changes. Finding the secret sensitive places he'd begun to know, the valley between her full breasts, the juncture of hip and thigh, the sweet, sensitive spot at the nape of her neck. He lifted her up in his arms and she straddled him, wrapping her legs tightly around his waist.

Her mouth was warm and inviting and tasted of sweet summer tomatoes. Her tongue met his and he moaned. He loved the feel of her, of her blossoming body pressed against his. His whole body ached. He wanted her with a fierceness that shook him to the soles of his boots. But it was mid-afternoon, there were cowboys and wranglers and maids everywhere.

So staying away hadn't quite done it the way he'd planned. He thought that putting some distance between them would help him get over her. Instead it just made things worse.

"Do you know what you do to me?" he asked.

She didn't answer, but she knew. His obvious arousal pressed into the apex of her thighs could leave no doubt in her mind.

"You torture me," he said gruffly, pulling back to look into her soft brown eyes.

Mallory framed his face in her hands and tightened her legs around him. Love, marriage, they were not for her. Not now. Not ever. But Zach was here. So big, so strong, so real. She'd missed him so much, and she wanted him so badly. "Is this torture?" she asked, kissing his forehead, his sandpaper-rough chin, and finally his lips.

His answer was a low moan deep in his throat. He kissed her back. Their mouths fused. Their kisses were wild and frantic. All the tension that had built for the past weeks broke, and she forgot where they were. It didn't matter that it was the middle of the day and there were wranglers and maids likely to walk in on them at any minute. What had happened to the sensible Mallory? She was gone—and good riddance.

Her face flamed, her body temperature skyrocketed. "It's too hot in here," she said gasping for breath.

"If you can't stand the heat," he whispered in her ear.

"Let's get out of the kitchen," she pleaded.

"Your place or mine?" His lips brushed against her ear.

She shivered. Hot on the inside, cool on the outside. She pictured his big bed, the smooth sheets. The memories of the passion there lingered in her mind and would never be forgotten. "Yours."

He carried her through the house. Miraculously they saw no one on their way up the stairs and into his room. And no one saw them. He carried her straight to his bed. She couldn't wait to see his body, his long muscular legs, his potent arousal. She would die if she couldn't feel his skin next to hers, cooling her fevered body. She wanted, needed him to make her whole once again. Now. Kneeling in the middle of the bed, she pulled his shirt from his jeans.

Sitting on the edge of the bed, he untied her apron, pulled her stretch pants down and then her bikini panties. Gently he laid her onto the bed. Then he ripped his clothes off, buttons flying, and pressed his cheek against her womb. She melted inside. Sparks shot through her body. She struggled with her shirt, finally tearing it off along with her bra.

His mouth trailed kisses over her body, paying homage to her enlarged and oh-so-tender breasts.

"I didn't think you could be any more beautiful," he whispered, burying his face in the valley between her breasts. "But you are."

She flushed from head to toe. Her body responded in a way she'd never dreamed of. She was throbbing, pulsating, alive and aching in every pore. When he reached her thighs, he kissed her gently until she unfolded like a summer poppy. Then his tongue invaded her secret place, seeking the honey within. She trembled. She shook. There was nothing she could do but explode. She wasn't prepared for the eruption that rocked her body like a volcano that had been dormant much too long. He drew her to him, and she collapsed against his hard body, arms wrapped around each other.

He stroked her face, he kissed her eyelids. His callused fingers caressed her breasts, circling her pale, dusky nipples, admiring the way they peaked even now, worshipping her with his eyes and his hands.

"You are so lovely," he said under his breath. "I can't believe how responsive you are."

She smiled and buried her face against his chest, the crisp hair tickling her skin. Then she slid her hands down his chest to the nest of hair and found his masculinity, so large, so strong, so ready. She stroked the velvety smoothness, loving the feel of him, loving the way he groaned deep in his throat. Loving the way he moved in her hands, the power she had to make him throb. Wanting him more than ever, inside her, filling her, making her complete.

"Now," she whispered. "Please."

He answered her plea with a swiftness that made her gasp. His hands pressed hers back against the quilt. His thrusts were fast and furious. She gazed into his face, his hooded eyes and his mouth and she knew nothing could ever match this. She threw her arms around him and welcomed him by calling his name once again. She wanted it to go on forever, this ancient give and take, the thrust and parry, but he came much too soon and yet he could hold back no longer.

He shattered inside her and rolled over on his side, taking her with him. They lay there, whispering.

"You make me feel beautiful," she said.

"You are beautiful." He traced his finger around the outline of her cheek.

"I'm eight months pregnant."

"I know." His hand moved to the outline of her breasts and down to her belly.

She glanced at his clock on his nightstand. She sat up abruptly.

"I can't believe it's five o'clock. I told Tex I'd have the sauce ready for dinner."

"It doesn't matter," he said, his hand caressing her hip.

"It does matter," she said, rolling off the bed and searching for her discarded clothes. "There will be a dozen hungry wranglers in the dining room at six. And my boss likes to eat too."

"Tell him you had more important things to do than make spaghetti sauce."

"Nobody tells Zach Calhoun anything."

"Maybe it's time they did," he said with a lazy grin, watching her put her clothes on from the bed where he was still stretched out, completely naked.

She shook her head as she yanked on her pants, averting her eyes. He was so gorgeous, so sexy that it was all she could do to keep her mind on the spaghetti and not jump right back in bed with him. She smoothed her smock, picked up her apron and ran her fingers through her hair before she left the room without another word.

Zach lay flat on his back staring at the ceiling, feeling a shaft of pain in his chest. He didn't know what to call it but it came upon him at times when he thought about Mallory leaving. It could have been loneliness, though he didn't really know what that was. He was an expert at getting along on his own. And had been since he was ten. He thought he'd gotten over this obsession with Mallory.

He'd told himself he needed to put some distance between them. He made up reasons for traveling, for taking buying and selling trips. Lonely? He was mistaken. He'd conquered loneliness years ago. It couldn't be loneliness. It had to be something else. The taste of her lingered in his mouth and the memory of her body pressed against his, the look on her face when she climaxed, the feeling he'd come home when he entered her body. These things stayed with him and he was afraid he'd never forget them. Finally he got up and dressed for dinner.

Neither one mentioned that afternoon again. Neither mentioned anything much about anything except the impending arrival of her sister. He didn't know if she regretted it or was just trying to forget it as he was. Trying to prepare himself for her eventual departure, when he'd no longer find her in the kitchen or on the hill with her telescope or in his bed.

Her sister arrived on Saturday with her husband and two boys. He stood in the doorway with Mallory at his side.

"I can't," she whispered.

"Yes, you can," he said, giving her a gentle nudge.

She nodded, bit her lip and moved out into the driveway like a robot to greet them. He heard her sister shriek when she saw Mallory, saw her give her sister a hug, stand back, look at her and hug her again. He might have been mistaken, but he thought they were both crying.

The husband was unloading the car, the kids were running around, and Zach went out to introduce himself since it looked like no one else was going to do it for him. He was vastly relieved to see Mallory, once she'd hugged her nephews and her brother-in-law, was laughing and talking nonstop with her sister. He caught her eye as they walked through the house on their way upstairs and gave her an inquisitive look.

She smiled, still a little teary-eyed and nodded. Then when no one was looking, she put her hand on his arm and whispered in his ear. "Thank you," she said.

Other than that, he didn't see her alone or get a chance to talk to her during the weekend. Zach helped the boys saddle up two gentle horses, and he took the boys horseback riding while their father went fishing. They all went on a picnic, food courtesy of Tex. Mallory let them look through her telescope at the stars at night.

Zach took the boys up to the pond to skip stones and for the first time he seriously wondered what it would be like if he had a child. Someone who'd love the ranch as much as he did. For the first time, as he stood on the grassy bank with a smooth stone in his hand, with the excited cries of the boys ringing in the air, he could actually picture himself as a father. Yes, he'd always thought raising cattle was the most satisfying thing he could do. But lately he'd begun to wonder...

After they'd left on Sunday night, he found Mallory sitting in the padded swing on the front porch.

"They wore you out," he said, sitting next to her. "You did too much."

"No, you did too much," she said. "They had a wonderful time, thanks to you."

"What about you?" he asked, slanting his gaze at her, noting her flushed cheeks, her bright eyes.

"Yes," she said with a happy sigh. "I had a wonderful time, too. I can't believe it. Mimi and I got along better than we ever did. In our whole lives. I don't know why. Maybe it's called maturity."

"What did she say about your pregnancy?"

"She's happy for me, but she's worried, too. About how I'm going to manage on my own. But lots of women are single mothers and they manage just fine. I'm lucky because as a teacher I don't have a nine-to-five job."

"So you think you'll manage just fine," he said. He wanted to tell her that his mother, after being deserted by his father, didn't manage at all. But then Mallory was a competent person with a career. Maybe she would.

"Yes, of course." Mallory was proud of how confident she sounded. How steady her hands were, when inside she was shaking. Zach would never know how scared she was. Scared of the birth process, even more scared of how she would manage, finding someone to care for her baby, juggling her career with her child. And most terrifying of all, leaving the ranch and Zach behind, never to see either one again.

"Anyway," she continued. "You were a big hit with all of them, especially the kids. I hope they didn't get in your way."

"No. I got a kick out of them. They reminded me of me at that age. They never stop asking questions. 'How does a brown cow make white milk? Why do bulls have horns? Why do fish like worms?'"

"I don't know how you had the patience to deal with them. I know Mimi sometimes goes crazy."

"I don't know, either, but it was only a weekend. Full-time kids would be another matter."

"Right," Mallory said. "Full-time kids would be... Oh, Lord." Suddenly the enormity of single motherhood overwhelmed her in spite of her brave words.

Zach put his arm around her and drew her to him. She pressed her face against his shoulder while a tear ran down her cheek. She was so weepy, so emotional. He was so big, so strong, so reassuring. She felt as if he had enough strength for both of them. That if he held her tight enough she could draw on that strength. But if she did, then she'd never be able to get along by herself. She could get used to leaning on him, but that would be a big mistake. A mistake she'd live to regret when she was on her own again. It was bad enough she'd have to live with the memories of the lovemaking they'd shared. He'd call it sex, but she knew better. She was in love with him. God save her.

"I don't know what's wrong with me," she said under her breath. "I cry all the time, at nothing."

"Maybe it's because you're pregnant," he said.

"That's what Mimi said," she said in a muffled voice. "She was like that."

"Maybe everybody's like that," he suggested, stroking

her arm. Just the touch of his hand made her feel that everything would be all right.

"Including cattle?" she asked glancing up at his profile with his prominent cheekbones, his stubborn chin and broad forehead.

"Especially cattle. They have their ups and downs, too. Though I haven't actually seen one cry as much as you do. But it won't be long now. You'll have the baby, and you'll be back to normal."

"Walking instead of waddling. Wearing real clothes instead of pants with elastic waists." And living somewhere else. In town. By herself. She sighed and lifted herself out of the swing. Getting in and out of chairs and swings was getting more difficult by the day. Her due date was in six weeks and she was dreading it and looking forward to it at the same time. So what else was new?

"What did you think of Kent?" she asked offhandedly, bracing her hand against the post.

"Seemed nice. Said you were the one who introduced him to Mimi."

"Yes. I knew what would happen if I did. What always happened. He fell in love with her."

"Did you care?" he asked.

"Yes, I cared. I thought I loved him." She sighed. "Wrong again." She paused. "Mimi's pretty, isn't she?" she asked.

"Very pretty," he agreed.

"Charming and vivacious and slim, too."

He grinned. She was fishing and he knew it. "Not as charming and vivacious as you are," he said. "Slimmer maybe, but I like a woman with a few extra pounds."

"Thirty extra pounds?" she asked incredulously.

He didn't say anything, but there was no mistaking the desire that flared in his blue eyes. He desired her. She knew it. He'd proved it that afternoon in his bedroom. But she still couldn't get it through her head. She was huge and ungainly, cranky and emotional. He still wanted her. It was unbelievable, but there it was. It made her want to cry or laugh, or both.

But she couldn't make love with him again. It was hard enough to get through these next few weeks. She had to be strong in order to turn her back on him and walk out of his life. She turned and trudged into the house, feeling every one of the extra thirty pounds weighing down on her. At the same time she felt her spirits soar. Just knowing he cared about her. That's what pregnancy did to her. No, that's what *Zach* did to her.

Her stretch maternity leotard left nothing to the imagination. Mallory would have been self-conscious if the exercise classroom hadn't been filled with women who were also in their ninth month of pregnancy and also wearing revealing leotards. Along with their partners or coaches. Some partners were other women, some were husbands. Mallory suspected that none of them but hers were their bosses.

The class had been together for six weeks now. They knew a lot about each other, but they didn't know Zach wasn't her husband. In between classes Zach had read books on labor and delivery. Mallory was reading a mystery novel, trying not to think about labor and delivery and all the things that could go wrong. They hadn't talked about the future. In one class they'd watched a movie with a real birth and heard a lecture on C-sections, during which one coach actually fainted.

"Why are you so calm?" Mallory asked Zach during the exercise session as she turned her torso from one side to the other to strengthen her back muscles.

"Listen," he said, leaning against the wall. "There's nothing to worry about. I've delivered calves in the middle of a field in the rain, rump first, by myself. This kid of yours is headfirst, if we can believe the ultrasound the doc showed us. We're going to be in a hospital with a doctor and all kinds of equipment around. But if I had to, I could probably deliver it myself."

"As long as I have a calf," she muttered. And had her first contraction. She sat bolt upright on the pad in the middle of the room, her eyes wide. "Oh, my God."

"What, what is it?" he demanded, grabbing her arms.

"I think...I think...that may have been a contraction."

He took his timer from his pocket. The rest of the class stopped practicing their pelvic tilts and made a circle around her. The next contraction came five minutes later. Zach helped her to her feet. Her knees buckled and he carried her to the car, the whole class calling advice from the doorway and shouting words of encouragement.

"Don't forget the ice."

"Remember the baking soda."

"Got your timer?"

"Let us know."

Zach drove and timed her contractions at the same time. She wished she'd put her little suitcase in the car. She wished she'd thought of names for the baby. She wished most of all that it was all over. Everything was a blur, the cars on the road, the admissions desk, the nurses, the birthing room, the drafty hospital gown. But through the blur was Zach, wearing a green scrub gown, and with her every minute, talking her through the pain, wiping her face with a cool cloth, rubbing her back.

"Did you hear that? The nurse said you're dilated three centimeters."

"That's good. Is that good?" she gasped.

"That's excellent."

She grimaced.

"You can yell, you know. You can shout if you want. There's nobody here but me."

She yelled, she shouted and later, much later, when the doctor came and she thought she couldn't last another minute, she delivered a seven pound eight ounce girl. The doctor gave her to her "daddy" to hold.

He opened his mouth to say he wasn't the father. But no words came out. His mouth was too dry, as dry as the cotton swabs on the shelf. His heart pounded. The baby was so small, so light, so perfect. He clenched his jaw so hard he was afraid it had locked in place. He looked into the infant's blotchy, little face with its receding chin and boxer's nose, and he felt tears sting his eyes. She was beautiful. The most beautiful baby he'd ever seen. A powerful, energizing warmth surged through his heart and flooded his whole body.

Could this be love? It was. It had to be. He loved this baby. After all these years, he'd fallen in love with a baby! He looked at Mallory. Her hair was hanging in limp strands around her tear-streaked face. She had blue circles under her eyes. And she'd never looked more beautiful to him. Because he loved her. There could be no other reason. The realization hit him like the back of a barn door.

He hadn't cried when he was six and he fell off his bike. Yes, he had cried when his mother left, but he hadn't cried when he learned she was never coming back. He wasn't going to cry now. But he was closer than he cared to admit. He wanted this baby with a longing so fierce it shocked him. The longer he held it and felt the warmth of its tiny body the more he wanted it to be his. The more he felt it *was* his.

He gave the baby back to the doctor and the doctor gave it to Mallory. Who did cry. The tears rolled down her face as fast as he could wipe them away.

She gulped. "A girl? It can't be a girl."

"But it is," Zach said. "And she's beautiful. She looks just like you."

Cradling the baby in her arms, gazing into its face, she choked back a laugh that turned into sobs. Heartbreaking, heart-wrenching sobs.

"Stop," he said. "I know you wanted a boy, but girls aren't that bad. You'll get used to her."

"It's not that," she said, propping herself against the pillow and holding the baby to her breast.

"What is it?"

"I don't have a name for a girl."

Zach stayed overnight in the hospital, sleeping in the waiting room with another new father. As often as he reminded himself he wasn't the father, he couldn't shake the feeling that he was this baby's father. It started the first day he'd met Mallory when she'd fainted on his living room floor and he'd picked her up and carried her across the room. He didn't know she was pregnant then, but there was something there, something that bound him together with this woman and this child.

In the early morning he went to the nursery and stared through the glass at the babies, at *her* baby, with "Phillips" written on the side of the crib. It was insanely irrational, but he wanted that baby to have *his* name on her crib, and *his* name on her birth certificate.

But she wouldn't. She wasn't his baby. He had to get that through his head, because if he didn't, he was headed for a big disappointment on the day they left. Disaster was more like it.

The baby was a big hit at the ranch. So many of the staff came to see Mallory and the baby, Zach tacked a visiting-hours schedule on her door. Of course the hours didn't apply to him.

He walked in on her one morning a week later. She was sitting at her desk, wearing a red-and-white-striped smock over bright red stretch pants, her hair a halo of curls around her head. She was talking on the phone.

"I'll take it," Mallory said to the landlord. "I'll send you a check for the first and last and the cleaning deposit." She jumped guiltily when she saw Zach at the door. She didn't want him to hear, but he had to know she was leaving.

"What was that all about?" he asked with a frown on his face.

"I found a place to stay."

"You have a place to stay."

"Zach, I can't take advantage of you anymore. I haven't earned my salary for months. You can't go on supporting me like a...a charity case."

"That's not how I feel about you." He glanced at the crib where the baby was sleeping. "When are you leaving?" His voice was tense. The lines around his mouth matched the grooves etched in his forehead.

"On the first."

"That's too soon. You're not going back to work already, are you?"

"No, but..."

"Then you don't have to leave."

"I have to leave. I *have* to leave." She swallowed hard. If she didn't leave soon she'd never leave. It was too comfortable here, too perfect. This big, wonderful house, the staff who showered her with love and affection. If it weren't for Zach...she might stay forever. But she couldn't.

She couldn't live under the same roof with a man she was hopelessly in love with. With a man who'd been hurt too badly to ever love again. And was too stubborn to try. She'd be better off by herself, no matter how hard it would be to cope with a baby and a job, than to be constantly reminded that he could never love her, that he'd always prefer his ranch, and that he preferred raising cattle to kids.

"Why do you have to leave? To get back to 'real life'?" His voice reeked of sarcasm.

"You know why," she said. "I can't continue to be the assistant housekeeper. You don't need one."

She thought he'd refute that statement, but he didn't. He couldn't. He just stood there with his arms folded across his chest and glared at her.

"I just want to say," she continued, "that I appreciate everything you've done for us, for me and the baby."

Again his eyes wandered to the sleeping baby. The hard expression on his face softened, just a little, but she noticed. She noticed everything about him. "No name yet?" he asked after a long pause.

"No, I...I...haven't. Any ideas?"

"If it was a boy I'd suggest Aberdeen Angus or maybe Hereford."

She smiled. "He'd be the only kid in kindergarten named after a cow."

"But since she's a girl, how about Andromeda or Venus or maybe even Sagittarius?"

"Maybe I'll stick to something more ordinary."

"How about Annie?"

"My grandma's name. You remembered." Her lower lip trembled. "Annie. Annie Phillips. Do you like it?"

He liked Annie Calhoun better. But he didn't say that.

"I like it. She looks like an Annie. Well, now that we've solved all your problems..."

"Zach. You know why I have to leave, don't you?"

"No."

She took a deep breath, stood and faced him. If she didn't say it now, she'd never say it. "Yes you do. We both know why I can't stay here. This isn't my home. It's yours. When I came here I was all alone, scared to death of the future, but I'm not scared anymore and I'm not alone. It's time for me to go, Zach. You know it and I know it. If I don't go now, I'll never go."

She paused for breath. Her lungs had run out of air. Her face was flaming and her heart was beating like a drum. She waited for him to say the magic words. The only words that could convince her to stay. But he didn't. He never would.

The baby woke up and started to cry. As if she knew she was leaving the only home she'd ever known. Mallory lifted her out of the crib and patted her back, making soft soothing sounds.

Zach stood there for a moment, watching the sunlight stream in the window and pick up the golden strands in Mallory's hair. The sight of mother and baby bathed in sunlight was something he'd never forget. His heart was full to bursting with an aching sadness.

"Mallory, I'm asking you, I'm telling you...I want you to stay." He'd come as close to begging her to stay as he could.

Stubbornly, she shook her head.

He clamped his jaw shut so tightly he was afraid he'd never be able to open it again. There was nothing more he could say or do to make her change her mind. So he turned and left the room.

Mallory's knees wobbled so much she had to sit on her

bed for a half an hour holding the baby before she could stand again and put her back in her crib. The tears she'd held in check streamed down her face. She didn't know why she was crying. As if she'd really expected him to tell her he loved her and he wanted to marry her. Yes, and why not ask for the moon too, the moon and the stars and a big telescope to boot? Why not, as long as she was dreaming. Why not ask for it all?

She wiped her eyes, finally got up, did a reality check, and went to her desk to order a phone and electric service for her new apartment.

On Monday morning Cass took care of the baby while she packed her car. Out of the corner of her eye she watched the house, thinking that Zach would come out and say goodbye to her. But hoping he wouldn't. She couldn't take another painful scene, since she'd said her tearful goodbyes last night to the staff.

She'd barely seen Zach since she told him she couldn't stay, and she didn't want to see him again. She might give in. She might decide that life on the ranch was so good it didn't matter whether he loved her or not. She might decide that she just didn't have the strength to go. She crammed her boxes and suitcases into the car, muttering to herself. "You knew you'd have to leave. You knew it from the beginning. Now get in the car and go. Before you change your mind. He doesn't love you. He's not going to marry you. So don't keep looking back at the house, hoping for a miracle. It's not going to happen."

Cass came out with the baby and Mallory fastened her into her car seat. Now maybe she could get out of there before she did something stupid like changing her mind. She drove slowly down the driveway, her gaze drawn to the rearview mirror, knowing he wouldn't suddenly appear, knowing he'd seen enough women disappear down

that driveway and never come back. Knowing he didn't
care enough to tell her not to leave. But foolishly hoping...

Zach didn't watch her leave. He couldn't be a ten-year-
old kid again, losing the only person he loved, having his
heart broken again. He couldn't. He was afraid he might
lose it. He was afraid after all these years of learning to
control his emotions, he might break down and cry. He
heard her car, though. He knew she was gone.

He walked down the hall and stood in the middle of her
room. The crib was empty. Her bed was stripped. He sat
down on the mattress, feeling empty, as if he'd lost everything. He hadn't. He'd only lost his assistant housekeeper.
The ranch was still there. The ranch that he loved more
than anything. Only now he wasn't so sure about that. He
looked out the window at the vast fields and the herds
grazing in the distance. And he knew they meant nothing.
Nothing without her.

He bit his lower lip to keep from crying. He bit it so
hard he tasted blood. Blood mixed with tears, the tears he
could no longer control. She was gone. Gone out of his
life. God, he was an idiot. He had to get her back. He
couldn't get his mother back, he couldn't get his wife back.
They were gone, a part of his past. But there was the future. A bleak future without Mallory and her baby. He
would get her back. He had to get her back. If he got down
on his knees and begged her to stay she might come back.
If he promised her the moon and the stars and a high-
powered telescope to see them with she might reconsider.

He was on his way to the garage to get his car to go
after her, when he heard her car chugging up the driveway.
He stood in front of the house, openmouthed, unable to
believe his eyes. Before she'd even come to a stop, he'd

wrenched the door open. His heart was pounding. She got out and stood staring at him.

"I forgot," she said.

"Forgot your crib?"

"Forgot to read my horoscope," she said breathlessly.

"Don't bother. I know what it says," he said. "I memorized it this morning. 'You've been patient with loved ones lately. Even when they don't deserve it. Today they show their appreciation.'"

"I don't get it," she said, her lips trembling.

"Don't you?" He pulled her into his arms then, and crushed her to him. He held her so tight she couldn't leave if she'd wanted to. He couldn't stop kissing her, couldn't stop loving her, wanting her, cherishing her.

"I love you," he said. "I was coming to get you, to tell you I started to fall for you the day you fainted on my living room floor. Now I love you more than anything."

"More than the ranch?"

"More than the whole damned ranch."

"I don't care. I just want to be part of your life. I'll be your assistant housekeeper. Because I love you. That's what I came back to tell you."

"I don't want an assistant housekeeper. I want a wife and I want a baby."

A slow warmth spread though her body as the truth sank in. He loved her, he really loved her. "You're in luck," she said. "Because today your stars are in alignment and anything is possible."

"Anything? Even getting you to marry me, to be my wife instead of my housekeeper?"

She looped her hands around his neck and gazed up at him, unshed tears glistening in her eyes. "I'll have to think it over."

"Take your time. You have thirty seconds."

"Are there any perks that come with this new position?"

"I'm glad you asked. First there's the moon and the stars. And the high-powered telescope to watch them with."

"You're trying to buy me, aren't you?"

"Not just you. You and your baby."

"Our baby," she whispered in his ear.

"Our baby, our ranch and our future. Together, forever."

She sighed blissfully. "All this and the nebulae, too."

* * * * *

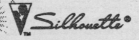

If you enjoyed what you just read,
then we've got an offer you can't resist!

Take 2 bestselling love stories FREE!

Plus get a FREE surprise gift!

Clip this page and mail it to Silhouette Reader Service™

IN U.S.A.
3010 Walden Ave.
P.O. Box 1867
Buffalo, N.Y. 14240-1867

IN CANADA
P.O. Box 609
Fort Erie, Ontario
L2A 5X3

YES! Please send me 2 free Silhouette Desire® novels and my free surprise gift. Then send me 6 brand-new novels every month, which I will receive months before they're available in stores. In the U.S.A., bill me at the bargain price of $3.12 plus 25¢ delivery per book and applicable sales tax, if any*. In Canada, bill me at the bargain price of $3.49 plus 25¢ delivery per book and applicable taxes**. That's the complete price and a savings of over 10% off the cover prices—what a great deal! I understand that accepting the 2 free books and gift places me under no obligation ever to buy any books. I can always return a shipment and cancel at any time. Even if I never buy another book from Silhouette, the 2 free books and gift are mine to keep forever. So why not take us up on our invitation. You'll be glad you did!

225 SEN CNFA
326 SEN CNFC

Name	(PLEASE PRINT)	
Address	Apt.#	
City	State/Prov.	Zip/Postal Code

* Terms and prices subject to change without notice. Sales tax applicable in N.Y.
** Canadian residents will be charged applicable provincial taxes and GST.
  All orders subject to approval. Offer limited to one per household.
  ® are registered trademarks of Harlequin Enterprises Limited.

DES99   ©1998 Harlequin Enterprises Limited

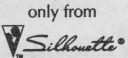

Based on the bestselling miniseries

A FORTUNE'S CHILDREN *Wedding:*
THE HOODWINKED BRIDE

by BARBARA BOSWELL

This March, the Fortune family discovers a twenty-six-year-old secret—beautiful Angelica Carroll *Fortune!* Kate Fortune hires Flynt Corrigan to protect the newest Fortune, and this jaded investigator soon finds this his most tantalizing—and tormenting—assignment to date....

Barbara Boswell's single title is just one of the captivating romances in Silhouette's exciting new miniseries, **Fortune's Children: The Brides,** featuring six special women who perpetuate a family legacy that is greater than mere riches!

Look for *The Honor Bound Groom,* by Jennifer Greene, when **Fortune's Children: The Brides** launches in Silhouette Desire in January 1999!

Available at your favorite retail outlet.

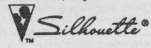

SILHOUETTE® *Desire*

COMING NEXT MONTH